Praise for Nikki Duncan's
Her Miracle Man

"Without a doubt, *Her Miracle Man* is unlike any romance novel you've ever read. This isn't a book; it's a journey through life, death, grief, and learning to live again. It is not lighthearted, it is not sappy, but it's original, touching, and you will be forever changed..."

~ *Guilty Pleasures Book Reviews*

"*Her Miracle Man* is written with a deep sensitivity to those who have suffered a loss in their lives. It is well worth the time to read this one. It's the first book I have read by Ms. Duncan and I can tell you it won't be my last."

~ *Fresh Fiction*

Look for these titles by
Nikki Duncan

Now Available:

Tulle and Tulips
Tangled in Tulle
Twisted in Tulips
Handcuffed in Housewares

Sensory Ops
Sounds to Die By
Scent of Persuasion
Illicit Intuitions
A Killing Touch

Whispering Cove
Wicked
Burned

Print Anthologies
Wild, Wet and Wicked
Burned, Bold and Brazen

Her Miracle Man

Nikki Duncan

SAMHAIN
PUBLISHING

Samhain Publishing, Ltd.
11821 Mason Montgomery Road, 4B
Cincinnati, OH 45249
www.samhainpublishing.com

Her Miracle Man
Copyright © 2013 by Nikki Duncan
Print ISBN: 978-1-61921-501-6
Digital ISBN: 978-1-61921-100-1

Editing by Tera Kleinfelter
Cover by Angela Waters

First Samhain Publishing, Ltd. electronic publication: November 2012
First Samhain Publishing, Ltd. print publication: October 2013

Acknowledgements and Dedication

To my editor, Tera Kleinfelter, your excitement about this story and your willingness to take on Indianapolis with Chaos and Destruction astounds me. We had a blast and I have a handful of adjectives to describe you. Funny. Smart. Talented. Generous. Supportive. Fantastic. Friend.

To Sara Megibow who gave me a new angle to consider and who put me in touch with Firefighter Richard Estep.

To Richard, your insights and information added a depth I hadn't considered. Thank you for the help in being accurate.

With tremendous gratitude I offer my thanks to Kelly and Daun at Ronald McDonald House in Indianapolis, Tom at Riley Hospital for Children Library, and the amazing PR team and administrative staff. Your willingness to talk with me, answer questions and share powerful stories touched my heart and made it possible for me to add legitimacy to this story.

To anyone who has dealt with the grief of loss or the delicacies of ill children, I hope I have done justice to the story of Jennalyn and Ryland, and I hope it adds a touch of light to your life.

Sincerely,
Nikki

Dear Readers,

Her Miracle Man began as a joke about the 12 Dates of Christmas and was intended to be a fun, light Christmas story. The moment I began working on the synopsis, however, I knew the story would be so much more than a joke.

Planning this story has taken me on a journey of research and discovery unlike any I've traveled before. I dove into the world of child illnesses, organ and tissue donation and even the intricacies of cadaver donation. I've met and spoken with so many people who've been more generous with their time and insights than I had hoped to imagine. Every conversation, every story and memory shared touched my heart and added the depth of a personal touch to this story.

While I have known the fear of a cancerous scare with one of my own children we were lucky enough to receive a clean diagnosis. The suffering of losing a child is something no adult should know, but I learned in researching and writing this book that the people who have lost the most are often the people who give back the most.

On a trip to visit Riley Hospital for Children in Indianapolis, Indiana, I had the honor of meeting some amazing staff from Ronald McDonald House. Their stories of patients and families, of sacrifices and victories, brought me to tears, touched my heart and reaffirmed my belief in the strength of the human spirit.

If you are familiar with the Circle City, you may recognize a few of the locations in this story. If you have ever had an experience with Riley or Ronald McDonald House, you will likely recognize the spirit and dedication of the staffs and volunteers.

I worked very hard to stay true to the places I've used in this book. The true-life Chief Medical Officer of Riley is often seen in the halls of the hospital. He may not know the patients as well as my hero, but the families and patients know him. The staff thinks of him by his first name, and it's obvious he's very well thought of.

Also, the red wagons mentioned in the story are real, as well as the fact that they can be sponsored in the name of a child. I hadn't known about them before my visit, but once I did I knew they had to have a role in the book. Their meaning and the stories behind each one are too important to be left out.

The biggest divorce from fact I've used within the framework of fiction is in regards to clowns at Riley. In reality, due to child safety concerns and administrative procedures, they no longer allow clowns in the hospital, but I do have one in *Her Miracle Man*. I hope, if you have a personal experience or connection with Riley, that you will indulge me.

It is my greatest hope that you will be as touched by *Her Miracle Man* as I have been.

Nikki

Chapter One

"That cake should have been here two hours ago." Water danced around the glass surrounding Jennalyn James. Her voice ricocheted off the rounded walls of the dolphin dome. Trying to stay calm, and hoping it was the dome's acoustics that made her sound less than in control, Jennalyn ran a soft rag over the fins of the sculpture in the center of the dome.

She wanted every surface to catch and reflect the blue, watery light to perfection. Who was she kidding? She wanted everything about the night to be perfect.

As she polished the bronze dolphin, two live dolphins drifted just outside the dome. Floating with grace, they watched her and the statue that danced on the tense tip of its tail. Did they view her as a mystery? Did they feel her anticipation? Or maybe—and it was an idea that sparked sadness—they recognized her.

With the idea of recognition came the memories of the times she'd stood in this exact spot with her sister. The zoo's dome had been their favorite place in Indiana. Her heart became a ponderous burden in her chest. Her eyes burned as her mind traveled back to the last time she'd come to the zoo. It had been a day designed for pleasure. Three short hours later pleasure had turned to agony.

She and Sabrina had stood with their fingers interlocked.

They had laughed and smiled while watching the dolphins dance and play. They'd seen the dolphin show so many times that they had recognized the pair as the youngest males. Their muscles rippled down their sides differently. The older of the two had a small scrape by his right fin. He had been Sabrina's favorite from the moment she saw him. Later they'd decided it was because of his stubborn streak his trainers spoke of. Like the dolphin, Sabrina had been quite resolute in her approach to the world.

It had been a perfect day. The kind of day they had tried to have at least once a month. The kind of day Jennalyn would never know again.

"Are you there?"

The young man on the phone pulled Jennalyn back to the task at hand. Cake. She hadn't received the cake. "Yes. How far away are they?"

"They were caught behind a wreck that closed down the highway," the man said apologetically. "They're currently on Meridian, about to turn onto Washington."

"Great." They had picked what was likely the busiest route available, but at least it was during the lull of the mid-afternoon.

"You're in the Dolphin Adventure Gallery, correct?"

"Yes. Thank you." Jennalyn checked her watch, recalculated her timeline for the afternoon, and then breathed a shaky sigh of relief. "Tell them to drive safely."

The success of this event meant a great deal to the family business she'd taken over. With tonight and one or two more big events she would finally be able to make some needed upgrades for the business. Starting with a new van and an inventory expansion of event supplies. If things went very well she could hire a staff to handle the setup.

Exiting to the left of the dome she found a new issue needing resolution. The crew who'd come in with the rented chairs and tables were setting up small, short, round tables where the bar and reception would be. They would be okay if she were putting on a tea party for children. Adults would be standing at them though.

"No! Those are the wrong tables."

A couple of heads popped up. She zeroed in on the potbellied man with his hair sticking out like he hadn't brushed it in a few months. The clipboard in his hand was the only thing remotely authoritative about him.

He paused, stared at her for a beat and then resumed his setup. "They're small rounds."

"I asked for tall bar tables. Not—" she motioned to the tiny table sitting before her, "—these."

"You asked for round tables."

Jennalyn pointed to the fabric room divider she'd had constructed from a pale blue, gauzy fabric with shots of silver and white running through it. It suited the room perfectly and was much easier to move than the traditional room dividers. "Behind that curtain are where the round tables go. *Large* round tables. For dinner."

She gestured to the part of the room where they currently stood. "Here is where I need tall bar tables for people to place their drinks or purses or whatever while they network. Standing."

"They can pull chairs up to these just as easily," the man argued.

"If we had ordered that many chairs and everyone was four feet tall, yes." She stepped closer to the man with a tight smile pulling at her lips. She tried to employ the theory about catching more flies with honey, but something told her nothing

13

was going to go over with this man without offending or angering him. "In the end, that is not what the client asked for."

"You want us to load these up?"

The work crew stopped mid setup and darted glances between her and the portly man. Some of their faces would have been comical if she weren't pushing the wire to get things in place before the event began. And she still needed to sneak away long enough to get herself ready.

"Yes, please. And in their place I would like the fifteen tall tables that are on the original order."

"Listen, lady..." The man stepped forward.

"No." She stepped forward. She hated when people addressed her that way. She hated when people addressed anyone with such disrespect and she wouldn't let it pass. "Do you have children?"

"Yes."

"Have you ever brought them to this zoo for a day of fun?"

"Of course."

"Then you listen to me." It took effort to not inject a bit of bite into her tone, but she pulled it off. "Tonight is a fundraiser for this zoo. The people attending are paying several hundred dollars to be here. They are the same people whose donations keep the entry costs low. Is it really so much to ask that they be able to stand with their drink rather than sit at kid-sized tables?"

The man's eyes darted around, looking anywhere but directly at Jennalyn. He almost looked as if he would dig his toe into the patterned carpet. He didn't. "I guess not."

"Then I would really appreciate it if you would get these tables switched out for the tall ones we ordered."

"Lady, do you know how many events we have going on

right now? It's nearly Thanksgiving and our staff is stretched pretty thin."

"Proper verification of the orders would prevent avoidable mistakes, which would ease some of the burden on the staff. I emailed a confirmation list."

"But—"

"I would prefer there be no tables at all, but my client made a specific request. I passed that request on to your company." She smiled, though she knew it held no warmth. "Should I find a new place for my business?"

"No, ma'am."

"Excellent." With that round won and with the man's crew scurrying to pack up the tables, she offered a suggestion. "Perhaps if you call ahead, someone at the warehouse can load another truck with the correct tables. You could even pass them on the road."

"Yes. That's a good idea."

After dealing with the tables, Jennalyn checked in with the bartenders setting up. Then she crossed to the back half of the room to place the reserved signs on the tables closest to the stage that had been set up to the left of the windows that looked into the dome. Two flautists would be playing throughout the night. One would be in the front half of the room and the other in the back.

They'd been in earlier to run through their songs and check their volumes to make sure they weren't playing so loudly they hindered conversation, but also to be sure they could be heard throughout the space. They would each wear an earpiece that would allow them to communicate about which songs to play next and when to take a break.

When she'd been planning the event with Evan, the head of public relations for the zoo, they'd considered bringing in a more traditional band. In the end, they decided the flowing notes of a flute would blend more smoothly with the classy mood they wanted to evoke. They'd planned a light menu with pretty touches to keep the theme going.

Jennalyn knew better than to think she would eat anything once people began arriving, so after working her way through the light switches again, making sure the lighting effects they wanted were set up correctly, she headed out for a quick bite at one of the concession stands. In the private room Evan had appointed hers for the night, she changed from her T-shirt, jeans and tennis shoes to an elegant black dress and heels that would allow her to blend more smoothly with the attendees. She touched up her makeup and fluffed her newly short hair before heading back to the event space.

Two hours later, as she hovered on the outer edges of the crowd, making sure the wait staff saw to everyone's needs and that nothing fell through the cracks, she nodded approvingly. The tables were correct and the cake, the amazing cake that should've been a crime to cut into, was in place. Like the sculpture in the dome, it was a masterpiece.

The four-foot dolphin, suspended mid-leap above gently rippling water, had people talking. No one cared about the mechanics of the clear wires extending from the frame that had been covered in fondant so it matched the room. They only cared about the beauty around them.

"Jennalyn." Evan slipped his hand into hers and squeezed. "You've done an amazing job."

"Thank you." She smiled into Evan's fun, green eyes that sparkled in his creaseless face.

"You deserve the thanks." He grinned with the mischievousness that alerted her to a scheme she should be worried about.

He had become one of her favorite people as soon as they'd started working together. They shared a sense of humor as well as a dedication to success in their careers. Best of all Evan was perfectly safe. He had zero interest in a sexual relationship with her. Even if he hadn't been gay she would have held him in the friend slot. She didn't have time for romance.

Evan continued, needing no encouragement to divulge what he had planned. "There's only one way I can show you how much we appreciate everything you've done to make this event perfect."

She turned away from scanning the room and focused fully on Evan. The outer edge of her right eye squinched a little as she attempted to predict what her unpredictable friend would say. Her attempt to brace herself eked into her tone. "Evan."

"I have someone I want you to meet."

The two ominous notes of the Jaws score played in her head. She knew what was coming. The two dreaded notes were replaced with two dreaded words.

"A man."

Yep. Just as she had expected. "Evan."

She tried to warn him. They'd shared enough apple martinis for him to know she didn't want to be set up. The family event-planning business had suffered too much while she had been taking care of Sabrina. With things finally on an upswing she couldn't afford the distraction that came with a man.

Even if she had the time, the hanging grief of loss didn't give her the heart. "Don't think for a second that I want you to set me up."

He cocked a hip with a fist lightly planted above the blinged-out belt he was never without. "Don't you think I know that?"

"I would like to, but you're being overly dramatic. That always gets me a little scared."

"Try to introduce a friend to a potential client and she gets all suspicious." Evan rolled his eyes as he grabbed her arm and propelled her through the crowded room. "Where's the appreciation?"

"I have plenty of appreciation." Relief flooded her. A personal referral was exactly what she could use, especially to the kind of client who could afford to attend a five-hundred-dollar-a-plate fundraiser. "Tell me about this potential client."

"He's the CMO of a local hospital and has wanted to plan a special series of events for some patients who are finally healthy enough to enjoy them." Evan smiled and nodded to people they passed, all the while talking low enough that their conversation was almost private. "Until now he's had to prioritize his focus on other things."

"What kind of patients?"

"Kids." Evan inclined his head toward a small group of people mingling near a bar table.

A handsome man and a pretty woman, maybe in her fifties, faced Jennalyn. Recognition settled uncomfortably. The man's smile was pleasant. The woman she remembered from her visits to the Ronald McDonald House in Riley. Amanda loved the house that love built and all that it stood for. She lived for the pleasure of making sure families had what they needed while their children were in the hospital.

Amanda was a wonderful person, but neither she nor the man facing Jennalyn held themselves as if they considered themselves powerful. The man with his back to her did. After seeing the woman, Jennalyn knew who the man was from his perfectly trimmed hair to the way he stood with understated power.

Then he turned.

He wore a black suit. The matching tie had a single row of red dots made from silk thread. At six foot two he was taller than her by seven inches. Square jaw and high cheekbones, blonde hair with silvery eyes that smiled when he smiled, the man robbed her of breath.

Ryland Davids.

Evan made the introductions, but Jennalyn heard nothing. She could only recall the times she had seen Ryland walking the halls of Riley Hospital for Children. He was an executive as dedicated to the comfort of the families of his patients as he was to the patients themselves. He was personable. So much so that he had been the one to offer warmth when her world went dark.

Jennalyn's head tingled. The sensation was subtle at first. Then it grew until the entire surface beneath her skull became a tingling mass. The pressure of memories swamped her and had her resisting the urge to turn and flee.

"Jennalyn?" Evan's questioning concern and the weight of his hand coming to rest at her waist pulled her from the morass. "I would like you to meet Ryland Davids, Brad from his PR department, and Amanda from Ronald McDonald House."

Amanda smiled a smile that said she remembered Jennalyn and that she understood how painful this reunion could be. The sympathy had Jennalyn resisting the urge to crack her knuckles. It was that look that had kept her from returning to the hospital as a volunteer. Turning from it, she faced Ryland.

He stepped forward with a hand extended and a gentle smile that curved his mouth and crinkled the edges of his eyes. "Jennalyn."

She flattened her palm over her chest where heat was spreading deeper. She'd seen him often, met him twice. The first meeting, she'd found him on the floor of the hospital library. In his expensive suit, in front of some amazing stained glass windows, he'd sat on the thick rug that covered a marble floor with his legs crisscrossed. He and Sabrina had broken away from their seemingly serious conversation.

He'd looked up at Jennalyn with the same gentle smile. It had stolen her breath then too.

In the water-themed banquet space, with her heart filling her throat, Jennalyn moved her hand into Ryland's. An electric jolt shot up her arm and had her jerking free.

Rubbing the palm of her still-tingling hand with her thumb, she searched for her voice. When she managed to push words up her lump-filled throat, she was proud to hear that she sounded somewhat level.

"Ryland."

"It's... You look... You look good." His guarded greeting suggested that he too remembered their last meeting and he found this reunion equally awkward.

The second and last time she'd met him... He'd sat across Sabrina's bed holding one fragile hand while Jennalyn held the other. Then, after Sabrina had slipped off to join the angels, when Jennalyn wanted to curl herself around her sister, desperate to keep Sabrina's body from turning cold, he'd rounded the bed and offered her comfort until long after the nursing staff had taken Sabrina away. Jennalyn could still hear her own grief echoing in that room.

Tears scalded Jennalyn's eyes, but she wouldn't let them fall. Her hands shook. The stress of the day, being back at the zoo, seeing Ryland and having the memories resurface all became too much. The strength she'd spent the last eleven months building up crumbled. Pinching her lips together, she held in a sob and backed away several steps. She couldn't stay and not break.

She fled.

She had been intrigued by the project Evan had mentioned. A series of events, even small ones, for a single client could more than put her where she needed to be to upgrade the family business. But working for Riley Hospital would require her to go to the hospital. She wasn't that strong.

Ducking her head, searching for privacy, she fought back the threatening tears and wound her way through the sparkling and laughing crowd. The exit was close, but not close enough.

Seeing Ryland again scraped away the scab that had thinned in the dome. Unshielded, the grief she'd thought she'd put behind her rose. There was no way she could take on a job for him. Anything involving the hospital would mean she would likely see some of the patients and families she'd gotten to know during their time there.

She'd grown to love those families, and they stayed in contact via email. She knew what had happened to the children Sabrina had grown to call friends. Some had lost the fight, some still fought, others were now on the road to a healthy life. She missed them all, but never agreed to meet-ups.

Swallowing tears, she pushed through the exit and stepped into the empty hall. Rubbing her chest and counting her breaths, she headed for the thankfully empty dome.

No.

She couldn't look at Ryland Davids.

She couldn't work for the hospital.

She couldn't relive the pain and loss.

Chapter Two

A triple threat—grief and pain and loneliness—had snapped into Jennalyn's large brown eyes. Her spunky hair with fun streaks, the flirty dress that curved her body and artfully applied makeup failed to serve as strong enough armor. The instant shadows darkening her eyes spread across her cheeks, removing the vibrant pink glow until all that remained of her beautiful complexion and spirit was a pale shell.

Ryland recognized the emotions and knew they were something she wanted to deal with in private. He had no right to follow her, other than the promise he'd made too long ago. Neither could he ignore her agony.

It had been seeing him that had taken her back to the day she'd lost her sister. That was the bitch about grief. It had a brutal way of sneaking up and biting the bereaved in the heart.

People who faced what Jennalyn had generally found reasons to hang around the hospital. Or they left and never returned.

The ones who returned and volunteered said it helped them remember the good parts of the loved one they lost. Or they simply wanted to make sure other people facing similar stresses had everything they could need to face each day a little more easily.

The ones who never returned found it too painful to face

the grief and loss. Seeing other people go through what they had gone through reminded them too vividly of their agony.

Ryland understood the motivations of both. And though he understood why Jennalyn had been one of the latter, a part of his heart broke each time he thought of her and Sabrina. He had thought of them often over the last several months.

Since hanging up his white coat, Ryland hadn't sat with a patient or family member in their last moments. That he'd been in Sabrina's room at the end hadn't been a coincidence. The magnetism of her optimism had pulled him in when he'd have been safer in his office. She hadn't been a patient long, but watching the way she fought against the degeneration of her brain cells, watching the way she fought to retain her memories and faculties while those cells died, had inspired him.

She'd become a favorite distraction when he needed a break. She'd made him laugh, and though he never told her, she had reminded him of his daughter.

Elise.

Even in her last moments, Sabrina had shone with a spirit of giving so strong he'd rarely seen its equal. She and Jennalyn had smiled at one another as she breathed her last breath. "Don't mourn too long," had been the last words to cross her smiling lips. The words, the smile, filled with such strength, did nothing to ease Jennalyn's heartbreak. Or his.

Neither had his holding Jennalyn after. No. Holding Jennalyn had only accomplished one thing. It had allowed her into a part of his soul where he should never allow a patient. It had reminded him of all the reasons most hospital administrators maintained a professional distance. Getting too close made making the tough decisions impossible.

He hadn't stopped to visit with a patient for more than a couple minutes since. Professional distance didn't stand up against the stark reality of seeing Jennalyn.

Just as she had in the hospital, she tugged at his heart with nothing more than a wounded look. She aroused his need to provide comfort and he wanted to think it was that need that propelled his steps through the room to follow her. Comfort, if he were able to offer it this time, would come a little later. He had a different agenda, thanks to a promise he'd been enticed into making to Sabrina.

Stopping at the end of the short tunnel that led into the dolphin dome, he sent a silent plea for Jennalyn to understand what he'd done to whatever god would listen.

Head held high, shoulders not shaking, she stood near the middle of the dome that extended into the dolphin tank. Her arms were wrapped around herself with the only visible movement being the subtle slide of her fingertips as they slid fractionally back and forth over her sides. More obvious was the grief that filled the air as effectively as the water filled the tank beyond the dome. One crack of the protective shell and there would be a flood.

Ryland felt it as clearly as the dolphins on the other side of the glass seemed to. Four sentries looking on with an eerie sadness, they hovered just beyond the glass. It was as if they shared a connection with her and understood her need for companionship from a safe distance.

Ryland rubbed a hand over his heart. He should turn away, make his delivery later, but it had to be done. In the inside pocket of his jacket sat the reason he'd followed Jennalyn. The promise he'd made to Sabrina had already waited too long.

Shoring up his defenses for another emotional blow, he stepped forward. Speaking softly, so he didn't scare her, he placed the tips of two fingers on her shoulder. "Jennalyn."

She didn't jump or turn to face him or stiffen beneath his

touch. There was a single sign that she heard him. That was a minor halt in her breathing. The halt lasted one beat, barely measurable, before the gentle rise and fall of her breaths resumed. "Go back to the party, Mr. Davids."

"I'm not much in the party mood."

Even their whispers bounced off the acoustically charged walls. His whisper, unlike hers, was more fact-filled than grief-stricken. He was no stranger to her pain, though. Hoping to offer encouragement, maybe a little strength, he eased a third finger onto her shoulder and took another step closer. With each inch closer he fought the urge to move in and wrap her in his arms.

He could kiss her, distract her from her pain. The vision snapped as clearly into his head as it had time and time again in dreams. The remembered feel of her in his arms beckoned a dark corner of his heart into the light. It persuaded him to hold her until her pain passed. Perhaps the kiss would get the desire for her out of his system. The risk wasn't safe for either of them so he ignored the emotional persuasion.

"You're missing out on some great networking opportunities for your hospital."

"There are more important things."

"Like following me?"

"Yes." He stepped around her, wanting, needing, to face her directly. "I'm sorry seeing me brought back your pain."

When she finally looked up it was with a gaze clear of emotion. No hurt. No anger. No nothing. "It never leaves."

I know. He wanted to say it. To let her know he truly understood her grief, but his experiences weren't important at the moment. Only she mattered. Her and her loss.

"When I heard you would be here," he continued, "I

worried… I almost didn't come."

"Why?" She challenged him in the same monotone that gave nothing away. "Because you sat with me after Sabrina died?"

Deep inside, she couldn't feel as matter of fact as she pretended. Not with the way she'd left the event. He knew how grief worked. How it spent years upon years messing with its victims.

"I had to see you."

"That's not at all contradictory."

He smiled at her sarcasm. She was shielding herself. He only hoped those shields were strong enough. "Call her. Don't call her. See her. Don't see her. It's a circulatory path I've traveled in my mind for the last several months."

She stared at him.

He stared at her while his mind wandered for a moment back in time.

But she'll be alone. I need to make sure she finds a way to be happy again. Will you help me? Sabrina's request had caught him by surprise, but he hadn't been able to deny the sweet girl with energy-sparked eyes.

A single statement had been all he needed to fall under Sabrina's spell. Now, here he stood before her sister, terrified that their plan wouldn't work quite how they'd hoped.

"I didn't want my appearance to cause you pain." Taking the disc from his pocket before he could turn back, Ryland offered it to Jennalyn. "But I had to see you. I had to give you this."

Her eyes flashed to the disc before returning to his. When she spoke it was with the same guarded monotone she'd used since he joined her in the dome. "What is that?"

"It's a message from Sabrina."

Jennalyn's head notched higher, as if she stretched through her spine. "What?"

"She asked me to help you stop grieving." Lifting Jennalyn's hand, he placed the disc in her palm. He didn't release her hand, though, after her fingers curled around the disc. "To do that, she left a few DVDs with me."

A blush touched Jennalyn's cheeks. It had nothing to do with her makeup and everything to do with the anger that popped in her eyes. "You've had discs of my sister this whole time?"

The tone of her question made him feel like a young boy being called out by his mom after breaking a major rule. She even had him wanting to duck his head and mumble his answer. He resisted. "Yes."

"And you're just now saying something?"

"Yes."

"And you're only giving me one?"

"I considered sending them before."

"But?"

"But, I chose to honor Sabrina's last request."

Jennalyn's eyelids froze open. Her head jerked a little to the right as if he'd slapped her. He'd known that last bit would hurt, but it had been unavoidable. He wasn't going to lie to her.

"What's on it?"

He shook his head.

"Do you know?"

He nodded once. He'd memorized Sabrina's messages as he'd helped her record them.

"But you won't tell me?"

He shook his head again. The messages would batter the barriers of self-protection Jennalyn had erected. "You'll want privacy when you watch this."

Privacy and likely a day or two for emotional recovery.

Jennalyn set her glass of wine on the square coffee table that had been in her parents' home, now her home, longer than she could remember. Nicks, stains and water marks scarred the surface as firmly as memories of her family scarred Jennalyn's heart. They would never be erased and she would never want them to be.

Rolling her neck, she tied the belt of her "I Believe in Santa" robe Sabrina had given her years earlier. Crossing her feet beneath her, she sat anxiously on the center cushion of the sofa and stared at the television. The DVD player was ready. The remote waited on the cushion beside her.

A single click of a button would have the DVD player closing. Then she'd hear whatever Sabrina had to say. She'd hear the message Ryland had held on to.

After taking a long swallow of the wine and returning the glass to the table with an increasingly shaky hand, Jennalyn held a deep breath and pushed play. The DVD drawer closed. Sabrina's face filled the big screen.

"Is it on? Are we ready?"

"Yes."

No. Jennalyn argued with Ryland's unseen response to Sabrina's slurred question. The brain damage she'd suffered in the car accident that killed their parents had turned her sunny tones into increasing slurs. With more brain cells dying each day, her too-short past fuzzed. Then she began losing her memories.

Sabrina had always maintained a brightness though, and it was evident as she settled more comfortably into the chair in the hospital library. She'd quickly claimed the spot as her favorite, especially after the staff had decorated the Christmas tree with books and colored lights.

"Hey, JJ." Sabrina smiled into the camera. It was a little timid, as if Sabrina was unsure of herself. The idea was an odd one, because uncertain was one thing Sabrina had never been. "You're probably mad at me for asking Mr. Davids to hold these messages."

"A little." Jennalyn didn't think twice about talking to her sister in the TV while tears burned her eyes.

"I thought... I thought you'd need some time."

"Eleven months, Sab?" Eleven months was more than *some* time. And what made Sabrina or Ryland think they had the right to determine how long she had to wait before seeing the DVDs?

"You told me not to be sad or angry that I was going to die. And I'm trying not to be." Sabrina sniffed away a tear. "When I can remember, I miss you and my friends, but I also remember what you taught me."

"What's that?" Jennalyn asked.

"You've said a lot lately that bad stuff happens. That we can't live in fear of it. You told me there was joy everywhere. Even in the hospital."

Tears coursed down Jennalyn's face despite her smile. She remembered telling Sabrina that. She'd hoped to offer comfort with the advice—for both of them—because the thought that she'd never see Sabrina's smile again, or hear her precious and wounded voice... Watching the video of her baby sister settling in for a lecture was oddly funny.

"Try not to be mad at Mr. Davids if he's kept his promise. He's sweet and doesn't want to upset you, but I've thought a lot about this."

"About what, Sab?"

"If you've kept the family business, I want you to take the job he's offering."

"He hasn't offered me a job." The point wouldn't matter to the video before her, but she couldn't stop herself from talking to her sister any more than she could stop herself from hoping to hear a little laughter. Of course, there was nothing funny about Sabrina's being gone.

"I was reading one day and heard... Okay, I was eavesdropping."

"I told you to stop that."

"You told me to stop that."

Sabrina's acknowledgement came at the same moment as Jennalyn's chastisement. Jennalyn laughed as her baby sister went on.

"But he has this idea. It's perfect. He's perfect. You're the perfect one to help him."

"That's a lot of perfection, Sab."

"That's a lot of perfection, you'll say, and it is. You're also perfect for him, but you won't let yourself see that for a while. You may not even admit how hot he is."

No. I know he's hot.

"Sabrina." The camera shook a little as Ryland chastised her sister.

Sabrina grinned and kept going. "He wants to plan a month of miracles for some patients. During Christmas because it's a hard time to be in the hospital."

"I can tell her the plans later, Sabrina," Ryland offered from off screen. His voice sounded thicker than normal, as if the idea of what he was doing with Sabrina was getting to him.

It certainly got to Jennalyn, but in the way that had her tears drying and her anger withering. Whatever her sister and Ryland had cooked up, she wasn't going to miss the chance for more DVDs of Sabrina. She would just have to find a way to avoid the hospital as much as possible.

Sabrina shook her head. "He wants to do stuff like days where gifts are delivered to every kid in the hospital or outings to someplace special or maybe something for the families." She swept a hand over the book in her lap.

Jennalyn's gaze dropped to the coffee table where the same book, *Soul Bound* by Mari Mancusi, sat. Sabrina had always had a book with her. *Soul Bound* had been her latest choice with her saying it was more fun to think about a vampire's dramatic life than her own.

"Personally," Sabrina continued, "I'd like to see you do a book event."

"Of course you would," Jennalyn slipped in. Meeting her favorite authors had been a dream of Sabrina's. They had talked with the Make-A-Wish Foundation, but before it had been pulled together Sabrina had been gone. With one dream unrealized, now she was asking for a new one.

"JJ, you probably haven't been back to the hospital since I died. I understand that, but you can't hide forever." Sabrina broke for a moment to take a few breaths. When she began again she sounded a little quieter. Sadder. "Promise me... Promise me that you'll go back. Help the kids and their families have a happy holiday."

"I don't know if I can." *If I'm strong enough.*

"Christmas was your favorite. Remember the fun we had. Share it with someone else."

"I don't exactly love Christmas anymore." Jennalyn talked to the screen as if her sister would answer.

It had been just before the holidays when she'd lost Sabrina. With the last of her family gone, she had no reason to celebrate. Decorating, shopping and baking no longer held the same pleasures. In fact, the only thing she'd pulled out last Christmas had been her robe. The only thing she'd wished for was a miracle Santa hadn't been able to grant.

"Don't live in your grief, JJ." Sabrina's plea lingered in her eyes until the screen went black. A moment later Ryland's face filled the screen, but he was no longer in Sabrina's room.

"I know hearing this from Sabrina this way isn't going to be easy for you. I tried to talk her out of it, but she's a determined little girl." He shook his head and released a soft laugh. It was nothing more than a single puff of air escaping through his nose, but it said so much about how quickly Sabrina had gotten under his skin. "I barely know her, but already I love her as if she were my own sister. I don't have it in me to deny her wishes, so if you're interested, I have a list of events I'd like to have you plan. Sabrina says you're amazing. I suspect she's right.

"I'm sorry for the hurt this causes you. I hope you'll call me."

With nothing more from Sabrina or Ryland, the screen went blank. Staring into the blackness of the television, Jennalyn wondered how Sabrina had come up with this plan. How had the sweet girl who'd never been able to keep a secret kept this one, especially near the end when she hadn't always had control over her thoughts and words? More importantly, Jennalyn wondered how she could think for even a moment about denying Sabrina's wish. Even Ryland had been unable to.

It would cut her heart to shreds to go back to the hospital, but Ryland's last statement had said it all. Because of the love Sabrina inspired, her wishes were impossible to deny.

Chapter Three

Ryland sweated beneath the heavy makeup, pokey wig, oversized shirt and pants held up by suspenders. The short time of discomfort was worth the smiles on the faces of the kids gathered around him in the main entry of the hospital as they watched him balance on a therapy ball while juggling stuffed bears. Occasionally he would toss a toy high into the air, so high it flew up to the height of the second floor balcony. The kids would all look up, watching and wondering when and where it would fall. If he threw it just right he could have it land in the lap of a child he knew would love it. Then a nurse would toss him another and he would keep the act going.

"Rylie!" a little boy in the front of the crowd cried out. "Show us a magic trick."

With a little flair, Ryland tossed the remaining toys he was juggling to the kids and jumped off the ball. Squatting, he did a duck walk toward the little boy. It wasn't easy in the giant shoes, but he was getting better at it. "What kind of magic trick would you like to see, Nicholas?"

"You know my name?"

"I do." Ryland smiled behind the mask of his makeup at the little boy who had recently been admitted for a defect in his heart.

As a hospital administrator, he still walked the halls. The

immersion into the hospital kept him aware of how policies were working, it helped the staff relate to him, and it aided him in carrying the needs of the staff, patients and their families into policies and procedures.

Since Sabrina, though, he no longer stopped by patient rooms for visits, and he didn't engage in conversations with them if he saw them in the public places. But neither could he make himself stay completely away from the kids, so he instead hid behind his alter ego, Rylie the Rowdy Clown. Through watching kids during his shows, and stories from the nurses, he learned about the patients.

"So, do you have a favorite magic trick?"

Nicholas thought for a moment before his smile bloomed. "Can you pull a rabbit from your hat?"

Ryland nodded. Pulling a hat from his trunk, he squeezed it in his hands to show the kids that he couldn't possibly hide a rabbit inside the soft hat. Then, wiggling the fingers of his glove-covered hand, he slid them inside the bottom of the hat and pushed a soft bunny out. The children laughed as he made the hand puppet dance. Then they gasped when Nicholas looked down to notice a stuffed white bunny sitting in his lap.

Bowing, Ryland swept his gaze over the crowd as he planned for one last trick. When his eyes landed on the latest newcomer to his show, a new excitement charged his plan. He immediately shifted gears.

"Kids, I have one last trick to show you. It's one I need some help with."

A chorus of "pick me" filled the lobby and floated up the open ceiling. Ryland shook his head and waved a hand dramatically.

"For this trick, I need a special volunteer." Sweeping his hand back and forth over the crowd a few times, studying the play of emotions on Jennalyn's face as he did, he stopped and pointed to her. "You. Sweet lady in the back."

The kids moaned their disappointment. Jennalyn shook her head and backed away two steps.

"Come now, sweet lady. Help me make these kids smile."

She shook her head again, but her gaze swept the faces that had turned to watch her. *Come on, Jennalyn. You can do it. Don't let us down.* She must have heard his silent plea, because she finally nodded and walked his way.

As she passed a little girl sitting in a wagon with red, wooden slats for sides her step faltered. Her gaze went to the license plate on the back with hope lighting her eyes. It was a look he saw often on the faces of families who'd lost loved ones. It was a look that told him she'd sponsored one of the child-centric transports in Sabrina's name. She was looking for the license plate that claimed it as Sabrina's wagon.

The light died. It wasn't Sabrina's wagon.

Widening his smile, even more determined to see Jennalyn happy, Ryland pitched his voice a little higher than when he'd last spoken. "As my lovely assistant makes her way up here, I want you all to be prepared to laugh. Are you ready?"

Cheers and applause erupted.

Jennalyn smiled at the kids as she wound her way through them. It was the same gentle smile she'd flashed the night before at the function. And like last night it didn't quite manage to extinguish the sadness touching her eyes. He would see her smile for real before A Month of Miracles was finished.

"What are you going to do with me, Rylie?" she asked as she set her bag, scarf and coat aside.

"I need you to help me with a few chores."

"Okay." She drew out the O as if she didn't trust where he

was going with the act. He knew she'd seen it before though. It had been one that always made her laugh.

"First—" he picked up a watering can and pointed to a large planter he'd set up before the kids came out, "I need you to water that plant."

Jennalyn shrugged and headed to the plant. Watching the kids sitting right in front of it, she tipped the can and poured the water over the artificial soil. The water flowed through the hidden tubes and poured onto the floor just in front of the kids Jennalyn watched. As it always happened, the kids shrieked and scooted back, laughing.

Jennalyn chuckled. Her smile broadened.

Rylie marched over to her and snatched the can away. "It wasn't nice of you to try to get those kids wet, lady."

Playing along, she shrugged dramatically, cocking her head to one side. "I wanted to see if they were really paying attention."

"Tsk-tsk." Rylie scolded her, shaking his finger back and forth in front of her face. "I think you should apologize to them."

Jennalyn bowed her head and knelt before the kids. "I'm sorry you almost got wet. Though I have to say I think it's his fault." She pointed over her shoulder at Rylie and pitched her voice in a loud whisper. "He likes to play pranks."

"Lady!" he exclaimed. "I thought you were sweet."

"A clown's first mistake," she taunted as she stood and turned back to face him. "Asking for a random volunteer."

"We shall see about that. Before we do, why don't you wipe up your mess?"

"Fine. Do you have a rag I could use?"

She remembered this act well. She embellished it better than he'd hoped, adding an excitement to it no other volunteer ever had.

"I do." Reaching into an oversized pocket, he pulled out a rag.

Jennalyn took it and began to walk toward the wet spot on the floor. The towel that had cleared his pocket had a piece of fish line hooked to it. As she moved a few feet away more rags began coming out of his pocket. Each rag was separated by another length of clear wire, sort of like fishing line but thinner and less shiny, so the effect was a row of rags floating in the air between him and Jennalyn. He gestured wildly for the kids to look at what she was doing. Pointing to the rags, tossing his hands up as if he had no idea how she was doing it and then crossing his arms as if resigned to wait until she got a clue. When she didn't turn around, but instead made a show about blotting up the wet spot on the carpet, the line began pulling at his pants.

Ryland danced in his spot, making the rags wave more wildly. The kids howled with laughter until finally Jennalyn turned to look at him. He stopped dancing immediately and flattened his hands on his chest, shaking his head. Clearly the floating rags were all her doing.

"Naughty clown." Jennalyn wasn't buying it though. Carefully working the twine attaching the rags so it stayed taut until she had plucked each rag from the air, she moved back to him. Stopping right in front of him, she turned to face the kids.

She didn't want to be in the hospital. He had seen that truth on her face when she had walked in, but she was putting her brave face on for the kids. The seriousness that had ruled her at the fundraiser was making way for the sense of humor he had seen her share with Sabrina. Rather than finding pleasure for herself though, she was doing it for the sake of the kids. It told him she was the kind of woman who would bend to the point of breaking if it meant making someone else happy.

"Sweetheart," she said to a little girl watching shyly from the edge of the group. "What's your name?"

"Bria." Shyness filled the little girl's smile.

"Can you please come help me?"

Bria hesitated before finally moving forward. When she was standing at Jennalyn's side, looking up with a shy twinkle in her smile, she asked "What do you want me to do?"

Jennalyn dropped all but the dripping towel at his feet and pulled his oversized pants farther away from his waist. "Hold these out please."

"Oh, sweet lady. Please don't do that," he pleaded. The kids cheered her on.

The smile he'd hoped to see twinkled in her eyes as she looked up at him and proceeded to wring the towel out.

The water, more than he'd imagined the one rag could soak up, dripped down the front of his slacks.

The children laughed and applauded.

Jennalyn let the wet towel fall into his clown pants and stooped low to address Bria. Again she spoke in the loud whisper that included everyone. "There was a lot of water on the floor over there."

Bria nodded. Ryland didn't like where this could be headed, but he stood still and watched.

"Do you think Rylie is wet enough?"

Bria shrugged.

Jennalyn turned to the other kids. "Do you think he is wet enough?"

"No!" came the chorus of adolescent yells.

"Wait!" Ryland protested. "No one really got wet."

"But they could have," Bria whispered.

Jennalyn grinned as if the girl had made her tremendously proud. "You are absolutely correct. They could have gotten very wet indeed."

"Sweet lady, I implore you to be kind."

Jennalyn ignored him, instead talking only to her partner in watery crime. "Why don't I hold this?" She took hold of the waist of his clown pants. "You go get that watering can."

"No, sweet ladies. Please don't do that." He danced around, but Jennalyn's hold on his pants hindered escape.

Bria smiled a little more boldly as she went for the watering can. Returning, her smile grew bolder with each marching step. She offered the can to Jennalyn, but instead of accepting it Jennalyn bent to Bria and whispered in her ear.

Ryland took the moment to beg a little more. "Please don't wet my pants."

The children laughed harder.

Bria's smile became a grin. She looked up at Ryland and brazenly lifted the can. With a side tilt of her sweet little head, the shy child tipped the can and poured the rest of the water down Ryland's pants.

"Oh no!" He danced in place as the water seeped through his trousers, making them stick to his legs. "My pants are wet."

Bria's hand shook as she began laughing. When she dropped the can and bent over clutching her stomach, Jennalyn knelt at her side. Bria's joy swept over the room until almost everyone was clutching their sides. Even Jennalyn shook with her laughter. A moment later she sank onto the floor and pulled Bria into her lap. Both laughed until tears spilled from their eyes.

Feeding the fun, Ryland danced and exclaimed more loudly

about his wet pants. He lamented that they stuck to him. That people would think he messed himself. His audience laughed until they cried and moaned that their sides hurt. And though he was aware of everyone, his focus was on the woman holding a patient at his feet.

She had drawn the girl from her shyness for the moment and in return, the girl had led her into some fun.

Being wet, having his tricks turned on him, needing to rethink how he dressed beneath his clown suit... None of it mattered. All that mattered was Jennalyn's presence and her smile. He had pulled off the first promise to Sabrina.

Male pride had him promising himself he'd do it again, because when Jennalyn James smiled she went from pretty to sexy.

Jennalyn watched the kids head back toward their rooms and though she tried to stop herself from looking at the wagons that passed she was helpless against the compulsion. Too big to use the fun alternative to wheelchairs, Sabrina had always walked around the hospital. She had loved the wagons though.

One night, a few weeks before she passed away, when the halls had gone quiet, Jennalyn had hunted down a wagon and pulled it into Sabrina's room.

"Hey, Sab, I brought you a surprise."

Sabrina rolled over in the bed. Her glazed eyes shifted between Jennalyn and the wagon for an instant before clearing. When the healthy part of her brain clicked on the who and what of the situation her lips curled up into the increasingly crooked smile.

"You're taking me for a ride?"

"Yes." Jennalyn grabbed the Christmas robe that matched

her own and helped Sabrina into it. After settling her sister into the wagon and putting pillows beneath her legs where they hung over the rails, she pulled Sab into the hall.

When they found a hall long enough, Jennalyn moved into a jog and then slid to a stop at the end. Back and forth they ran. Playing. Laughing. Sabrina delighted in every moment. Jennalyn wished the moment could have lasted forever.

"Bye, sweet lady." Bria's soft voice pulled Jennalyn from the past.

She knelt and accepted a hug from the little girl. The smell of strawberry shampoo and powder wrapped around her. Sweet. Comforting.

Jennalyn had struggled to maintain her composure from the moment she spotted the hospital entrance. The chilled, fall air had been powerless against the heat of emotions that had flushed her face. The struggle had eased minimally while she played with Bria as the girl's generous spirit slipped inside between the beats of her heart.

The heat of emotions she'd dodged began to rise again with Bria's soft arms hugging her. It was the first embrace she'd accepted since Ryland had held her. Pain, like she'd stayed too long in the cold and now the bone-deep freeze was beginning to thaw, filled her. So did relief. She felt more than grief.

"Bria. Thank you for helping me."

As Bria walked away the light from the bright and airy entrance struck her hair, affecting a sort of halo. Like so many times before, Jennalyn was amazed by how little the entrance, even filled with patients, felt like a hospital. The air was clean, but not in an overly disinfected way. Fresh, it made her feel hopeful that other kids and families would be luckier than her.

Large and small, farm animals and wild beasts mixed in with characters from popular kid shows to line the support beams near the ceiling. Glass, bullet-shaped elevators overlooked the lobby as they whisked patrons to their destinations. Bronze statues and benches placed among the cheery foliage lining a small pond gave the place the feel of an indoor park. The clown, currently watching her with his painted smile, lent the place a feeling of fun and vibrancy.

"You were a lovely assistant," he said as the last children moved away.

His voice, unlike during the show, was no longer disguised with fun and excitement. Now it carried the warm and gentle tones she recognized as Ryland's. Tilting her head, she studied him a moment. With closer study she began to see beneath the makeup, wig and funny clothes. Rylie the Rowdy Clown was Ryland the hospital CMO.

As the truth sank in, so did the memory of dumping water down him. She'd soaked the man she was relying on for a job. Not just any job though. The job that would establish her as a front-runner in the event planning business.

Fan-stinkin-tastic.

"Ryland." She wanted to close her eyes and drown herself in the small pool of water nearby. Instead, she forced her head higher and met his gaze directly. "I'm sorry about the water."

He shrugged as if it didn't matter. Beneath the makeup his face muscles never twitched, which made her wonder if he was really relaxed and uncaring about his wet clothes, or if he was just good at hiding his anger.

Hopefully the former.

"You made the act better." He motioned with his head toward the administration offices.

She took it as a sign to follow, so she grabbed her bag from where she'd dropped it earlier and went with him.

"Luckily I keep a change of clothes here." He talked casually as they headed past his assistant and into his office. "I just need to rethink my undergarments in the future."

"If I'd realized it was you—"

"You would have held back." Shaking a finger at her, he headed into a bathroom attached to his office. He was silent for several minutes. When he spoke his voice was muffled. "If you'd done that the kids wouldn't have enjoyed the act near as much. For me, hearing their laughter is like thunderclouds parting after a storm."

An image of the sun cracking through darkness blinked in her mind. It was a beautiful thought and it had been exactly how she felt when Bria and the kids laughed. "You're right. I still shouldn't have pushed as far as I did."

Ryland came to the door with his makeup smeared. He'd stepped out of his clown suit so all he wore were his wet pants. There was something improper about having a business meeting with a half-dressed man, though it proved one thing. Sabrina had been wrong about her not noticing how hot he was. The man was...divine.

"You were perfect, Jennalyn."

Trying not to focus on his naked torso, thinking his half-painted face was safer territory to study, Jennalyn locked her stare with his. Amid the splotches of color she found a complete calm. And honesty. And generosity.

The pain of a thaw moved through her again. She rubbed her chest.

Could he really be that okay with her soaking him? Or was he simply being nice because he felt sorry for her? "Pouring water down the pants of a prospective client isn't what I would consider a sound business move."

"The only business being transacted at the time was fun."

He leaned against the doorjamb and wiped the rag over his face. "And you, Jennalyn James, were having fun."

I was! "That is not the point."

He didn't argue or respond as he went back to the bathroom. Jennalyn walked to the breakfront cabinet along one wall. Twenty-one picture frames, all sterling silver with a small red wagon in the bottom left corner, held pictures of kids. No two pictures were the same, but they all showed signs of the kids being ill. An infant's photograph was the center point of the pictures.

A few minutes later he returned with his face clean and a fresh change of clothes on. With each button of his shirt he buttoned she felt the propriety of the meeting slip back into place. His next words shattered her hope that he would shift gears to straight business.

"Fun is exactly the point when a clown's around." He motioned her to the guest chair in front of his desk. When she sat he lowered himself into the one beside her. "Fun and forgetting all the sadness life slaps us with is exactly the point. Even if it's only for a little bit. "

"Of your act, or of my presence here?"

"Both."

"Are you asking for my help because of Sabrina?"

"No."

"Really?" She didn't know why she was arguing with him. His act had carried her beyond sadness many times. She'd never realized it was Ryland who eased the misery of so many. Including her. And now he was asking her to help do the same.

"Really."

"But Sabrina's DVD—"

"Got me thinking more seriously about the idea." He

reached out and grabbed a red file folder from his desk. "I've made some notes on what I would like to see happen with A Month of Miracles."

She flipped the folder open and was surprised to only find a short list of names. By each name was their illness, a hobby and a number. She almost asked about the details of the family, but as quick as the thought occurred it was dismissed. The outing wasn't being planned for the family. It was being planned for the kids.

"The patients on that list, and their families, have waited too long for the happiness and healing they're finally getting."

"And the numbers?"

"Those indicate how many people will be going on the outing, not including you and me."

"Wait. You intend for you and me to attend all of these events?" If the idea was to provide the family with a dream day they didn't need her shadowing them. She was the least fun person in Indianapolis these days.

"You have to make sure things go perfectly." He shrugged as a smile curled the left side of his mouth. "I have to pay the tabs."

She wasn't entirely comfortable with the idea of hanging out with Riley patients. Who was she kidding? She was entirely *un*comfortable with the idea. She would just have to find a way out of them.

"You said twelve events. There are only ten names here."

"Yes." He watched her carefully, as if he was gauging her reaction to each word. The scrutiny was a bit disconcerting, but she wouldn't be intimidated by it.

"I'm open to ideas on the outings," he continued, "with a few more specific requests."

"Okay."

"A few families of the listed kids have become largely involved in Ronald McDonald House. I would like to do something amazing for the house in their names."

With Christmas on the horizon and visions of the big house during the holidays fresh in her memory, she practically saw plans unfolding into fruition. "Sounds doable."

He nodded. "My final request is that we close out December with a truly special party. The kids on that list and their immediate families will be invited."

"That could be a pretty big party." Ideas whirled in bright strands of grandeur in her mind. From the small and intimate to the big and rowdy.

"Which is part of what makes it special."

Emphasis hung on the word *part*. It was there only for a breath, yet it was unmistakable. He had something up the sleeve of his perfectly tailored shirt.

"How do you know I'm the right person for this job?"

"I saw the work you put into the zoo fundraiser."

"That was one job."

"You've done others."

"Have you been watching me?"

He nodded. Once. "A Month of Miracles is yours to plan if you want the job."

The lack of answer had her stubborn side pushing her to demand more. Her professional side won. "You aren't going to check out other planners or price shop? Or quiz me on how I work?"

Was she trying to talk him out of using her?

"No." He angled his head so his chin was slightly down with

his eyes remaining up and on hers. "Are you trying to talk me or yourself out of this?"

"Aside from that not being smart business, I don't like the idea that you're showing me favoritism because of Sabrina." She didn't like the idea at all.

"A little of both then." Ryland answered his own question, tapped the file she still held and stood. "You can keep that, and when you decide to take the job let me know."

Chapter Four

"Mr. Davids, thank you again for..." Gavin's voice trailed off as he indicated the stadium filled with shades of Colts blue and Cowboys silver.

"Call me Ryland, and again, you're welcome." Ryland looked around the stadium much like Gavin, but he looked for Jennalyn. She'd been secretive about today's event and refused to ride with him. She wouldn't always win that fight. "You deserve this."

Fans were heading to and from the bathrooms and concession stands while the players returned to the locker rooms for a break and pep talk. Nachos and hot dogs, soda and beer. Curses and screams, laughter and cheers. It had all filled the sunny but fall-chilled air for the last hour and a half.

Lung capacities were tested with each interception of the ball. Friendships were made. Memories were treasured.

No fan, though, would remember the day as vividly as Gavin Ross.

One touchdown in one PeeWee football game was all Gavin would have the pleasure of making. He'd collapsed in the end zone when a damaged heart valve gave way, and with it a dream of playing ball. Practices and his undiagnosed heart murmur had proven too much for his body. By the time he was admitted to Riley, he had advanced endocarditis and was in need of a transplant.

Too weak to do much of anything, the last five years of Gavin's life had become a series of hospital stays, home seclusion and several failed attempts at valve replacements. The boy, now seventeen, had never lost his love of football. No matter how sick he'd been, if the Colts were playing he watched the game. Even his room at the hospital, from the door to the interior, had been transformed into a miniature stadium during his stays.

Rubbing a hand over his chest, where he likely had a gnarly scar from his multiple surgeries, Gavin watched two large groups of people form on the sidelines of the field. As guarded as he'd always been in the hospital, afraid to hope for the best, the smile he'd shown off all day never faltered. "I'd given up on the idea of getting to ever *see* a game."

"Some dreams are worth the wait. I hope this one was."

"It is." The teen nodded. "And this... This makes me want to work at Camp Riley. I want to help other kids learn that they're not defined by their physical situations. That there's hope for something better."

Before Ryland could respond, a woman stepped away from the sideline and walked along the fifty yard line to center field. Her more recently red streaks had been turned Colts blue to match her scarf and the jersey that hugged her subtle curves. Jennalyn had changed her hair for the occasion, and it only made her more charming.

"What's going on?"

Ryland shrugged and studied Jennalyn.

His blood coursed a little faster. Anticipation was only part of the cause. Jennalyn, despite the distance, made an impression. *What is she up to?*

At center field, she stopped. When the crowd of people

who'd been at the sidelines with her had marched out and assumed their spot, she turned and looked directly at Ryland and Gavin. The camera zoomed in on her face so anyone looking at the big screen might think she looked directly at them.

A proud smile curved her lips but it was the one that didn't fully penetrate the grief in her eyes. He found himself missing it as she raised the microphone she held. Without a word from her or the announcers, the crowd felt something coming. A pulsing hush fell over the stadium.

After a small swallow that rippled along her throat, Jennalyn spoke. "Thanksgiving is only a few days away. In the stands today is a young man who has a reason to be truly thankful for the first time in five years."

The big screen's view shifted.

Gavin's face filled it.

Shock registered for a flash before his smile became more stunning. He looked at Ryland who simply pointed to the field and shrugged. Jennalyn continued as the groups of people on either side of the field walked out, obliterating the yard lines with their bodies.

"Gavin. You've fought to survive the last five years. You've seen your dreams suffer and you've missed out on some big experiences." The emotion in Jennalyn's voice was ripe in the speakers. That, more than her chosen words, captivated everyone.

Some of the people who'd marched on the field with her turned. "You've missed attending school with your friends."

Gavin's jaw dropped as he leaned against the rail to study the faces of the people on the field. Looking around as if he couldn't decide where to look or how to act, he laughed.

"Your friends and their families have missed you." A second

portion of the group turned. "Even your teachers." And a third. "They've never forgotten you or given up hope that you'd get better. To show their support and happiness for your recovery, they've arranged a little something for you."

Jennalyn walked off the field, and from somewhere among the lines of people a bass voice boomed. "Hut. Hut."

Rhythmic claps and "huts" resounded as the group moved and reshaped their lines into letters. L-O-O-K L-E-F-T.

Gavin followed their direction to find himself looking at Blue the Mascot, and Jim Irsay, the team's owner. Laughter was replaced by a slack jaw as the kid slowly rose to his feet. He looked back and down to Ryland. "You knew about this."

Ryland shrugged. He'd only known about the game, but he could play along. "I believe they have something for you."

The camera followed Gavin as he edged in front of Ryland and moved toward Blue and Jim standing at the end of the row. Jim shook Gavin's hand and passed him an envelope. The game's announcer took over the speech.

"Gavin, you've just been handed Colts season tickets and locker room access for life. We're thrilled to have you as a fan."

"Seriously?"

Blue nodded, shaking his whole head. Jim shook Gavin's hand and smiled. "We're serious. Your story reminded our team how fragile life is and we wanted to celebrate that. Congratulations on your health."

"Thank you. I..."

Gavin's mouth formed words that wouldn't come.

"Hut. Hut." The unseen bass voice came from the field, saved Gavin from his thoughts as a shuffle of activity caught his attention.

Gavin's friends moved into a new set of words that had

several people in the crowd wiping their eyes. W-E L-O-V-E Y-O-U.

Gavin was still grinning twenty minutes later when the football game resumed. The time passed quickly with nearby fans coming over to congratulate Gavin. Each time he responded with "Thanks, I can't believe it." Ryland didn't time it, but he doubted sixty seconds went by without Gavin stating his disbelief.

"I can't believe you organized this for me."

Ryland shrugged again, in part because he didn't want the attention on him. And partly because he'd only known about the seats for today's game. "The woman from the field did the heavy lifting."

He'd witnessed the kind of moment he'd heard about from the kids and families who'd benefitted from the Make-A-Wish Foundation. The magnitude of what Gavin had just been given was proof that Ryland had hired the right woman to organize A Month of Miracles. His idea for Gavin had been to get him season tickets to the Colts. Jennalyn had apparently tracked down the owner and not only talked him into letting her use the field, but she'd convinced him to gift the boy with a lifetime of awesome days.

Her vision for Gavin's day had been motivated by her understanding of what the boy had faced during his illness. No other event coordinator could've added such a personal touch to the job. Ryland couldn't help but wonder how she would top it.

"Are we having a good time?" The feminine query broke him from his thoughts as Jennalyn dropped into the seat beside him. He'd hoped she would join them but each minute she was gone was a minute longer for doubt to set in.

Ryland smiled. His chest expanded, made room for his pleasure.

Gavin realized who she was and whatever guard he might still have vanished as he stepped over Ryland and pulled Jennalyn up and into a hug that Ryland was sure would crush her. "Thank you. Thank you for all the work you put into this."

Jennalyn's hands fluttered for a moment in the air before she patted Gavin's shoulders. After two pats she relaxed in his arms and returned the hug. "Your face lighting up the big screen reminded me of my sister when I surprised her with something. That was all the thanks I needed."

Ryland had only talked via phone with Jennalyn since she'd left his office two weeks before. It had surprised him to discover how much he had missed her. With her so close, his arms ached to be the ones holding her. He wanted to pull her in and tell her how proud and amazed she made him feel, yet her hesitation to return Gavin's affection was enough to know that she wouldn't want the touch. She wasn't ready.

And just when Ryland thought the moment would grow heavier, Gavin pulled back and asked, "So if you can get my schoolmates to do this for me, do you think you could talk them into doing all my schoolwork too?"

Jennalyn laughed and nudged the boy back toward his chair. "You sound like my younger sister trying to get out of math. She only loved reading. Used to say it was like watching a movie unfold from the pages."

"Now see, I'd rather do the math. Equations make more sense to me than sparkly vampires."

Again Jennalyn laughed. It was a spunky and fun sound that gave Ryland's heart a buoyant lift. The three of them spent the rest of the game talking and laughing and cheering the Colts to victory. Each minute that ticked off the scoreboard, Ryland saw a little more of the weight on Jennalyn's shoulders slip away. Sadness and seriousness lingered below the surface, it always would, but her smile was reaching her eyes a little more deeply. That alone made the day a victory.

Jennalyn fought the urge to strip and wrap herself in her robe for a long night of sulking. The day had been a great success. Gavin's friends had been amazing and needed little direction. The staff at Lucas Oil Stadium had been wonderful and easygoing about having an extra hundred people tromping around the private areas during the game. The players had been beyond gracious with their time.

She hadn't lied when she told Gavin that his smile had been thanks enough. That and his laughter had taken her back to the night she'd raced through the halls with Sabrina in the wagon. Like Sabrina had always been able to do, Gavin drove the darkness in her world away. But now he had gone home. The light of the day had faded and all Jennalyn saw was the empty home that should be filled with her family.

Knowing she was looking more for the sake of staying busy than hunger, she flipped through the pile of takeout menus she kept in the kitchen. Before Sabrina's accident, when her life had still been perfect, Jennalyn would have come home from work to cook dinner for herself and her fiancé. Family death and illness had a way of changing things though. Changing people. Bringing out their true colors.

Shoving the menus back into a drawer, she grabbed a wineglass and a bottle of red. She'd just taken the first sip when the doorbell rang.

She was a little taken aback to find Ryland on her doorstep. The jeans and Colts jersey were a departure from what she was accustomed to seeing him in, yet she liked the relaxed side of him. Liked it so much in fact that she'd struggled to focus on conversation with Gavin through the afternoon. Her mind continually went to Ryland and the warmth and power radiating around him.

"Ryland. What are you doing here?"

He glanced at the wine in her hand. The right side of his lips tilted up a little. "White just wouldn't cut it today?"

Swirling the burgundy liquid in the fat globed glass she shook her head. "It was this or a robe."

"You look great in jeans and a jersey." His gaze swept the length of her. "Though I wouldn't mind if you went for the robe."

"Cute." In silent invitation for him to enter, she stepped back and waved a hand toward the living room. "Are you going to tell me why you're here?"

"Gavin's never going to forget what you did for him today."

"Just doing my job."

Ryland walked around the room, looking at the photographs of her family. He traced a finger over the clay ashtray she'd made for her father when she'd been in kindergarten. He'd never smoked, but had always made sure it was out for everyone to see.

"Better than I could ever have hoped for."

"I'm glad you liked it."

"Loved it." He stopped his exploration of her home and walked slowly to where she stood.

Only inches separated them. He watched her. Silent. Unblinking. Intense.

Her blood heated beneath his scrutiny. The skin of her back itched along her spine. Was he going to kiss her? Did she want him to?

Her body canted toward him, answering the question for her. He was the first man she'd been attracted to since the last man she'd been attracted to. The heartbreak of that relationship had paled in the wake of her parents' deaths, but it had been real enough to breed caution.

"Ryland?"

"You're an attractive woman, Jennalyn."

The quiet resolve of his tone chilled her in an oddly exciting way. "Thank you."

They said nothing else. Neither did they break their locked gazes.

"I would like to kiss you."

The foundation beneath her feet trembled as if the house had been built on pillars of salt.

"Umm." Again her body canted forward slightly. Her eyes felt suddenly heavy, much like her brain.

Slowly, still not blinking, Ryland lowered his head toward her. Shivers of anticipation lightened her. The moment stretched, hummed, as his lips grew closer and closer. His breath brushed her lips, he was so near, but still he didn't kiss her.

"May I?"

"Kiss me?"

"If you think it wouldn't be too distasteful."

Please do. "I suppose it would be okay."

"I'll try not to disappoint," he whispered. But still he didn't move in for the kiss.

Instead, he took her wineglass and set it on the nearby table. The momentary break of his stare didn't ease the eagerness trembling in her. When he returned his attention to her, it came with a touch. He rested the tips of his fingers on her neck with his thumbs just barely brushing her jaw.

What was he waiting for? Energy flowed between them. Hers tingled along the base of her neck at the hairline. It was like her nerves were begging for him to touch her more fully.

On a soft exhale he closed the remaining distance. His lips brushed hers. Tentative to the point it was almost chaste. Still, an ember glowed brighter in her soul.

She stretched into him. He took the encouragement and deepened the kiss, though he kept his touch light while his thumbs stroked back and forth. Entranced, she parted for him, silently inviting him to kiss her more deeply.

He understood the plea and swept his tongue over hers. Another ember glowed to life, sparking even more. The heat of her blood warmed her skin. She didn't remember putting her hands on him, but the strength of his chest, the beat of his heart against her palm, grounded her. Then the erratic pace of her own heart invaded reality.

He'd carried her to a place she hadn't been for years. A place of abandon that would lead her into trouble if she wasn't careful. He made her want things she'd set aside long ago. Those wants were dangerous, because opening herself to them meant she'd have to open herself to everything else. And though she saw the logic of it, she wasn't interested in changing it.

She pulled back and grabbed her wineglass in hopes that holding something would help her minimize the trembling of her hands. Only time would restore steadiness to her breathing.

"I'm sorry," Ryland offered, watching her as closely as he had before kissing her.

"For kissing me?"

"No. Never for that." He swept his fingers along her jaw and smiled. "I'm sorry if I caused you any...discomfort."

"Life is one big *discomfort*." *One giant, miserable, seeping discomfort.*

"Yes, it is."

Something in his tone told her he knew how true the statement was. That same something told her the knowledge had nothing to do with his job. Needing to restore balance for the both of them, she asked again, "So why are you really here?"

Nodding once, he accepted the change of topic. "I brought you something. It's not as grand as the gift Gavin received, but I hope you'll like it. "

He pulled a rock from his pocket and handed it to her. She scrunched her brow and looked from the rock in her palm up to him. "You came all the way here to give me a rock?"

He shrugged. It was something she'd noticed him doing a lot of through the day, like he was a little uncomfortable having his generosity brought into the light. "It's peacock ore. It's pretty and vibrant on the outside and hard on the inside. It made me think of you."

"You think I'm hard?"

"Yes. No. Damn." He shoved his hands in his pockets, looking for all the universe like a boy who'd just been told he had to spend seven minutes in the closet with a girl. "I noticed a bowl of rocks in Sabrina's room during her last stay at Riley. She said you two had a thing for collecting them."

"So was this your idea? Or was this another of Sabrina's messages from the grave?"

"Not everything I do is motivated by a request from Sabrina."

"Sorry to offend," she said in response to the bite in his voice.

"No problem." Though clearly he had a little problem with what she'd said, because he moved toward the front door. "I do hope you know that while Sabrina might have kicked off the idea of you organizing A Month of Miracles, you got the job on your own merits. And Sabrina's ideas of us one day being together have nothing to do with the way you make me feel."

Following him to the door, touched by his sweetness and honesty, but not ready to ask him to stay, Jennalyn smiled. "Thank you."

"Thank you for a day of perfection."

Chapter Five

Jennalyn had only seen pictures of the crash that had handicapped her sister, but some pictures spoke more than a thousand words. And with the images in her head, it was never hard to imagine the sounds that had tainted the air that night.

One such sound was that of ambulance sirens racing toward someone in need of saving. The same sound ripped through the air as Ryland pulled into the parking lot of a fire station. She tried not to flinch, she always tried not to flinch, but the sound slapped Jennalyn with imagined images of the crash scene that had upended her life. She flinched.

Ryland was focused on finding a parking spot, but his keen observation skills meant he didn't miss much. His glance darted her way. "You okay?"

No. "Fine."

"You sure?"

"Yes." She hadn't sounded convincing to herself. How could she hope to fool the man who seemed to understand the darkest parts of her? Hell, it was that talent alone that played into her reasons for staying away from him as much as possible. "Have you spoken with Cooper and his mom today?"

"Yes."

Ryland scrutinized her from his periphery while slipping

his two-door coupe into a slot away from the front door, but not as far away from all the other cars as she'd expected him to. "You know there's a slot closer to the front door?"

"Yes, but I'd rather save that for Cooper and Debbie if they're not already here."

Chivalrous. Another charming characteristic to be added to the list of the man's attributes. Working with him, Jennalyn was beginning to see just how long the list was. That he let matters drop when he didn't believe her claims of being okay was another one.

"Today is quite different from a football game, Jennalyn." Ryland turned off the car and faced her head-on. "Are you going to be okay in here?"

"As long as they don't get a call." His sincerity had her responding with full candor when secrecy would have been more comfortable. She'd known going into this job that some moments were going to hurt worse than others. She was just hoping Cooper Faulkner's day would be as rewarding as Gavin's.

"If they do?"

"Then it'll be a shitty day for me. I'd rather focus on giving Cooper a perfect day."

"Deal. But if you need to leave, say the word."

"Thank you." Understanding and acceptance came so easily for him. Whether it was his intention or not, it warmed her every time she witnessed or received it.

Ryland said nothing else on the subject. Instead, he sat and watched her much as he had the night in her home. His brown eyes took on the same glint they had just before he'd kissed her. Before she'd been compelled to kiss him in return.

Beneath her coat and scarf, she became uncomfortably

warm. Almost hot. Breathing became difficult, as if her airways were constricted. Her tongue darted across her lips. His did the same.

She wanted to kiss him again. The want had grown daily since the last one until she wondered if her mind had over-embellished his appeal. No man could be so powerful that he made a woman want him with only a look. Yet, here she was. Looking. Wanting.

Shaking her head, clutching for the door handle, she scrambled from the car. A giant gasp filled her lungs with cold air. Then that same blast of cold had her hustling toward the front door.

When they stepped inside, Cooper and his mom were already waiting. Debbie was tall and slender to the point she looked like she needed to eat four-dozen cookies to put a pound on. Her straw-colored hair was thick but dull, and shadows lingered beneath her eyes as if they were trying to fade but worry kept them from fully vanishing. Clearly the woman had spent more time recently taking care of her son than herself. She deserved something for those efforts.

Cooper on the other hand, was a vivacious seven-year-old. He talked ninety-five miles an hour and had the chief laughing over whatever story he was telling. The shorter and healthier version of his mom's hair bounced as he chattered about a DS game and the cheats to get to the next levels. Sabrina had only gotten that excited about books, but regardless of the topic there was a special gift that came from seeing a child's happiness.

Jennalyn introduced Ryland to Chief Alexander and thanked him for the day.

"Zack is making a few last preparations and then he'll be with you."

Unlike many of the other kids on Ryland's list, Cooper hadn't been terminally ill. He had suffered life-threatening injuries in a car accident. The EMT who'd responded to their accident, Zack, had been able to stabilize his injuries and get him to Riley quickly. When Jennalyn had been setting the baking day up, Zack had told her his success was entirely the result of a child's cadaver being donated for testing.

A chill raced along Jennalyn's at the idea of a child's body being used for any kind of testing... It was agonizing to think about every time she remembered the conversation with Zack, but given that her sister's injuries had stemmed from an accident it was a need Jennalyn understood. The opportunity to study a child's anatomy carried with it the potential to save thousands of lives. The idea of someone's baby being cut into was just as powerful a motivation to not donate.

Even with Zack's unique experience and training, Cooper had spent six months in the hospital learning to walk again. But he was alive and as healthy as before the wreck.

"Where's my assistant baker for the day?" A big voice that Jennalyn recognized as Zack's greeted them before the man stepped into view.

He'd never topped five foot ten and was probably twice as wide as her, but every time Jennalyn saw him Zack seemed a little bigger. That was clearly a result of his personality.

"I'm here," Cooper piped up.

"Well, let's not stand around all day." Zack clapped his heavy hands and scowled good-naturedly. "We have baking to get done. These firefighters get nasty if they don't have enough junk food."

Cooper and Zack headed back down the hall with Ryland and Debbie following. Jennalyn hung back, pulling her cell from her pocket. Ryland, noticing she wasn't following, glanced back with concern. She smiled and waved him on with a signal to her phone.

He kept going and a few minutes later she was escorted into the kitchen by a grinning chief. "You're a smooth operator, Jennalyn James."

"I'm sure I don't know what you're talking about, Chief." She was chuckling as she joined Ryland, who sported an apron claiming that real men don't need antacids. Below the slogan was a cartoon of a firefighter whose heart stuck out from his chest with flames leaping off and wielding hoses to disintegrate a pile of antacids.

"Everything okay?" Ryland asked.

"Yes." She nodded to the apron and laughed again. "Do you know how ridiculous you look in that apron?"

"No more so than I look in a clown suit or with wet pants."

"Hmm." She looked around the kitchen. "I'm sure there is enough water around here for us to test one of those theories."

He took her arm and led her to the table with the mixer. "I'm sure you'll be staying away from all water."

She looked doubtfully at the large assortment of ingredients set out. "You think because I'm a woman that I'm better equipped for baking?"

"At least safer than you'll be at the sink."

"If you say so." She swiped her finger along the edge of a soft stick of butter and before he could move back she smeared it on his face.

Cooper howled with laughter from nearby, which of course had Ryland's alter ego coming out to play. Wiping the smear off his cheek, he turned to the boy. Waggling his finger dramatically before him, he rounded the counter. "You think that's funny?"

"Yes, but you're not supposed to play with the food."

Jennalyn snorted at the sight of the young boy chastising the hospital CMO, who currently wore an apron and a smear of butter. "Tell me, Cooper," she said to the boy. "Do you know how to do any of this?"

"Are you kidding? Mom and me have been baking forever."

"Well, aside from scrambled eggs, which are pretty tough to mess up, I'm better with a phone and credit card. Do you think you could help me out?"

"If you promise to not make messes."

He looked so serious about the request. As if he would write her off as a partner if she spilled some flour. Her dad and Sabrina had been the same way, while she and her mom had been challenged in the kitchen and had more fun starting food fights. The memory had her smiling and plotting ways to get the boy messy.

Debbie sat at the table rolling dough that Zack had already mixed up, but she did so in a pristine manner that told Jennalyn where Cooper had learned his manners. She would apologize later.

"I will do my best, Cooper, to minimize my messiness."

Ryland coughed. His gaze, that gaze that saw too clearly into her, called her a liar. It also said she could count on him to help play with the boy. Zack watched the interactions from the sidelines, silent and tough to read, but she figured she could persuade him pretty easily to join the fun.

What surprised her was that she wanted to play.

Jennalyn and Debbie stayed in the kitchen to keep an eye on the cookies and cakes while Ryland and Zack took Cooper to see the fire engines. Zack and the other firefighters, many of whom remembered Cooper from the accident that had badly injured him and taken his father, took great pleasure in showing Cooper the equipment in the ambulance that was used to save him. The boy had been having such a great time following the firefighters, climbing in the trucks and blowing the horns, that he didn't give a thought to his mom and Jennalyn staying in the kitchen to watch the goodies.

Besides, the women discovered a common interest in what they called a shared need for a personal stylist. Both claimed they were worthless in the coordination of outfits and knowing a good hairstyle when it hit them. Ryland could sort of see it in Debbie, whose focus had been on her son.

Jennalyn was another story. She was always put together from the tip of her spunky head to the toe of her shoes that seemed to always finish her outfits in a sensibly sexy way. He'd have argued the point if he didn't understand so well what it was like to be fashion-challenged.

Once he found a store with a staff that seemed to know what suited him and his job he hadn't shopped anywhere else. Aside from the junker clothes he used for chores around the house, they even outfitted him for his more casual days.

"Look at me, Mr. Ryland." Cooper's delighted demand drew Ryland's attention. Ryland turned from his thoughts to find the little boy standing in fireman boots with the heavy matching jacket pooling around his feet.

"You look ready to battle a dragon."

"Really?" Hope burst forth as if the kid saw his future riding on Ryland's next answer.

Ryland guessed it was more likely the boy's way of seeking a man's approval and pride. With his heart constricting as if a fist of iron squeezed it, Ryland knelt before the boy so he could look him directly in the eye. The kid watched him, waited. Ryland squeezed Cooper's skinny bicep gently.

"You standing here makes you a superhero. Build a few more muscles and you can take on anything. With or without this armor."

Cooper nodded once. It was the kind of nod one man gave another when women would share a hug. It was a strong, resolute nod that acknowledged and accepted Ryland's words while thanking him at the same time. It was the nod of a boy accepting his inner man.

"Cool." Shrugging out of the jacket, Cooper handed it up to one of Zack's counterparts. "But for now we should go check our baking. Mom is good, but Ms. Jennalyn..."

"Is not so good at the baking thing." Ryland winked. "She sure is sweet though."

They were still laughing over Jennalyn's shortcomings in the kitchen a few minutes later when they walked through the door. A paper plate smeared with buttercream frosting soared through the air. Ryland looked up just as it smacked him in the face. It landed more on his forehead and at the top of his head, but an instant later the rejected icing—Jennalyn's first attempt—was dripping down his face and into his eyes.

Ryland wiped the sticky sweetness off his face and stared into Jennalyn's eyes. "You are going to pay for that."

Cooper pointed at Ryland and howled. Debbie picked up a second plate and sent it flying. When the second plate connected with Cooper's chest, he laughed harder.

"Nice shot, Debbie!" Jennalyn's cheer bounced through the kitchen as she lifted another plate. She sent it soaring, again at Ryland.

He ducked and moved closer to the island counter. The plate smacked him on a shoulder. "Woman, you seem intent on making a mess of my clothes."

"Just having some fun. And I stayed away from the water, as per your request."

It had been a goal of his for Jennalyn to rediscover her fun side. He hadn't planned on it always adding to his dry cleaning bill.

Cooper and Debbie moved closer and closer to each other. Too close to actually throw plates, they settled on dipping their hands into the large bowl of icing to smear it over each other. Debbie's laughter was as uplifting as her son's, and her smile was as bright.

Ryland, determined to repay Jennalyn for the fight she'd started, ducked lower to take cover behind the counter. Low to the ground, knowing he couldn't be seen over the counter, he moved in the direction opposite to the one he'd been heading. If he could come up behind Jennalyn, he could grab a plate, tap her on the shoulder and...

She anticipated him.

When he rounded the corner and stood, she was waiting. A plate balanced on a hand, and a grin brightened her eyes. The grin distracted him. It was the first time he'd seen her smile fully banish her sadness. No doubt the moment would become a memory when the food fight was over, but it was a memory he would treasure.

"Jennalyn."

"Ryland."

"You're making a mess."

She tilted the plate from side to side. "It'll clean."

He scooped a blob of icing from his shoulder. "And my clothes?"

"Will clean too." Her nonchalant shrug contradicted the

gleam in her gaze. "Be grateful it's not one of your expensive suits."

Then, quicker than a blink, she lunged forward and smeared the icing all over his face and down his chest. Her laugh slipped like warm honey through Ryland's soul, brightening the dark corners he hadn't realized still existed.

Focused more on her fun—and revenge—he took one step closer and wrapped his arms around her. The icing-covered plate was pinned against him, but so was she. Excitement snapped at the base of his spine. Soft curves and warm sighs, the woman's impact on him became a wallop. If they were alone the moment would allow for a more intimate outcome. He was more than fine with this one. For now.

Holding her tight, he writhed against her, moving up and down her body with his until she was as covered in icing as him. Her gaze locked with his when he stopped moving.

"You enjoy that, Ryland?"

"Yes. You?" Easing in, lowering his head to hers, he watched her eyes dart around, taking in his face as she tried to brace for a kiss.

"More than I thought I might, actually." The pulse in her neck leapt.

"Good." His voice sounded husky even to himself. A weightless energy flowed between them until they were alone in a bubble.

"Kiss her!"

Cooper's call interrupted the bubble, but it wasn't enough to break their stare. Ryland grinned, enjoying the idea of kissing Jennalyn again. Easing closer, tightening his arms around her fractionally, he lowered his head. She drew in a breath. Held it.

He tilted his head and blew a warm breath along her neck.

She trembled against him. Yes, he definitely enjoyed the idea of kissing her again.

"Ryland."

Her plea was a whisper only he could hear. And only he could hear the loneliness beneath the thin layer of fun. He didn't want her sadness or loneliness to resurface so soon after she was laughing.

"Oh, JJ. I told you that you would pay." Surprise hit her eyes just as he tucked his chin to his chest and rubbed his icing-coated hair over her neck and shoulder. He wasn't sure if the vanilla he smelled was her perfume or the icing, but he knew that as of this moment it was his favorite scent.

"Excuse me."

Jennalyn and Ryland looked toward the door. "Chrissy," Jennalyn said, a little embarrassed sounding.

A curvy brunette, the assistant Jennalyn raved about, cleared her throat as she stood beside Zack. The firefighter's throat danced when he looked at the woman beside him. He said nothing though as Chrissy stepped into the room with an envelope in her hand.

"I have a delivery for Debbie."

"Right." Jennalyn pulled away from Ryland and headed to Chrissy. She wiped her hands over her hips as she went, but he wasn't sure that would be enough to keep the envelope clean when she fetched it. "Everyone, this is Chrissy. The angel of efficiency who's blessed my world."

"What could you have for me?" Debbie asked as she stepped away from Cooper, who was wiping icing from his face and licking his fingers clean.

Chrissy smiled and handed the envelope to Jennalyn, who turned to Debbie. "This day has been for Cooper, who has a heroic strength. I couldn't let the day pass, though, without recognizing the bravery of the woman who inspires Cooper to be who he is.

"This is for a day at Transformations Salon and Spa." Jennalyn passed the envelope to Debbie. "You're to get anything you want, all day, with no concern given to the cost."

"But..." Flummoxed, Debbie waved a hand toward Cooper. "I-I can't accept this."

Chrissy stepped forward with her card extended. "You let me know what day you have your appointment set for. Cooper will be well cared for until you get home."

Debbie's shoulders shook, and Ryland had no doubt that if he could see her face her chin would be trembling. He and Jennalyn had never talked about a day for Debbie, but Jennalyn had taken one look at the woman and known she needed time for herself.

He had been attracted to Jennalyn from the first time he'd seen her. As he experienced the beauty of her spirit, she became impossible not to fall for.

Chapter Six

Hours later—with the kitchen cleaned up from the icing fight—cakes, cupcakes and cookies of all shapes, sizes and flavors covered the counters in the firehouse. The place smelled like a bakery filled with peanut butter, chocolate, mint and vanilla. Buttercream icing stiffened everyone's hair, with the exception of Zack, who had captured the whole thing with a digital camera.

It had been a wonderful day that unexpectedly had Jennalyn recalling some of her favorite family memories. And for the first time since Kris had walked out on her, claiming she was too obsessed with trying to replace her parents in Sabrina's life, she saw a truth about herself. She hadn't been trying to replace her parents. She'd been substituting Sabrina for the child she'd always wanted to have. The child she'd planned on having with Kris before realizing how self-serving he was.

Staring at the stark reality, she still didn't feel that she'd done anything wrong. Sabrina had needed her. She'd needed Sabrina. There had been the same give-and-take relationship that any two people in a family would share. Husband and wife. Parent and child. Sister and sister.

It was the kind of bond she never would have had with her ex because he'd always been the taker. Never the giver.

She realized now that even in the beginning she'd caught

glimpses of his personality. The desire to be a part of something solid, something like her parents had had, drove her to ignore the parts of him she hadn't liked. Spending time with Ryland, watching him with the patients, she began to realize how grateful she was that Kris had left her. That he'd moved on to find someone better suited for the servant he sought. Not that she saw Ryland as a replacement in her life. Unlike the naiveté from years earlier, she now knew that not even a great man like Ryland would be able to fix the hole in her heart.

Her last chance for an amazing life had evaporated with Sabrina's last breath.

"I had wondered how you would top the Colts game." Ryland plucked dried icing from Jennalyn's hair as he walked her to her door. "I never would have expected a day of baking in a firehouse to be the day that would top it."

Her mind shifted back to the reality of the moment. To Ryland. "Your list said he liked baking. Then when you told me what station the ambulance had come from, it just seemed logical."

"Only to you. I would have gone for a pastry chef."

"I almost did. But I also know that firefighters are pretty well known for being good cooks. As it turns out, Zack put himself through college by working in a bakery."

"So it couldn't get any better than to have Cooper spend the day with an experienced baker who just happens to be the EMT responsible for him being alive."

"Something like that."

She glanced up at Ryland and flicked a dried fleck of icing off his shirt. After their almost kiss in the kitchen she had fabricated reasons to touch him. With every touch she tested her reaction to him. This time, like the touches before, her body hummed with awareness. It was low and suppressed, but she felt a difference in herself. She felt the desire to test her limits. To see if he was as attracted to her as he seemed to be.

"Was it something else?"

"I don't know." She pulled her key out and swung the chain in a gentle circle. "Spending the day with built men who know how to clean, cook and handle a hose isn't exactly a hardship."

She turned to unlock her door at the end of the statement, but she didn't have to be looking at Ryland to know he had stepped closer. The shift in the air, the way it pulsed with a tingling warmth, alerted her to his closeness.

"There are men who meet those qualifications without being a firefighter."

"Perhaps."

She opened the door, but before she could step inside, he grabbed her hips. Holding her in place, with her back to his chest on the front porch where her neighbors could witness, he lowered his mouth to her ear. "There is no perhaps."

Her eyes fluttered closed as the heat of his words slipped beneath the scarf wrapping her neck. The November chill vanished and her skin wasn't the only thing warming up.

"Boastful man," she teased.

"Invite me in, and I'll prove my point."

She suddenly felt as if she'd run a marathon in high humidity without drinking enough water. Weak legs, dizzy, flaming face, shortness of breath. Every symptom was accounted for, but so was the worry of what would happen if she gave in to him. Sabrina had said in her DVD they were perfect for each other. Was this his way of testing the theory? Was he simply going one step further in his promise to her sister?

"Ryland."

"Jennalyn." He brushed against her back, silently announcing his interest. "A night between consenting adults doesn't equate to forever." His fingers moved in tiny circles over her hips. "Just you and me. No work. No stress. No fears or bad memories."

A shiver started at the middle of her back and blew its way up to her neck. She tried to suppress the need to tremble, but her body won.

"Sometimes, giving in to a temptation is the best way to cure it."

She practically heard the smile splitting his face. He was getting to her and he knew it. Again, the shiver tracked up her spine. "I'm not sure that's going to be the case with you."

The honesty didn't surprise her. That she'd actually voiced it didn't really surprise her. That she trusted him enough to give him the truth—when she had guarded herself against pretty much everyone since her parents died—was the surprise.

Rather than push the moment, he eased back. The warmth that had filled her faded. With his hands still on her hips, he turned her. Glancing up at his bowed head, she met his gaze. She saw desire, hunger, but they weren't the ruling emotions. In the depths of his stare was a beautiful misery that was a kindred spirit to her own.

Tears burned her eyes, because in that moment, when she had expected things to take a sexual turn, he spun them to an emotional place. With a lingering glance, he offered her a glimpse into his soul. Then he did the same with softly spoken words.

"I understand you, Jennalyn." He released her, but only for the moment it took him to place a hand on her jaw. "I've felt your pain. Your loneliness."

Detailed explanations weren't necessary for her to know he

spoke sincerely.

"When you're ready to talk, I'm here." He kissed her. A gentle and sweet press of lips against hers was all it was. And though his touch quickened her blood, the heaviness in her heart came from his understanding.

"I'll see you in a couple of days." With a final press of his lips to hers, he placed a disc and a smooth stone in her hand and walked away.

Watching his retreating back, feeling the weight of the DVD in her hand, the moment of light flirtation and fun had passed. Glancing at the items he'd left behind, she unfolded the small paper sandwiched between the disc and gold-flecked stone.

Valued for its beautiful, shimmering sparkles, this goldstone reminds me of you. It's a scarcity as much as you are a rarity. You're both amazing. You're both in high demand.

Pressing the cool stone against her lips, hugging his words and the memory of his touch close, she went inside. She was still holding the stone against her lips, unable to put it down because of the sentiment Ryland put behind it, when she sank into her sofa. The bowl of rocks that had been in Sabrina's hospital room sat on the side table to her right. Picking up the remote and pressing play, she braced for whatever Sabrina had to say this time.

Sabrina wore her Christmas robe and sat in the chair in her hospital room with her legs curled up yoga style. She'd taken up meditation toward the end, and the chair seemed to be one of her favorite spots for it. Her hair was pulled into an intricate braid that Jennalyn remembered doing.

"Hey, JJ." Sabrina's lips curled into her sweet smile. "If you're watching this, you took on A Month of Miracles. I'm proud of you."

"You say that as if you made two sets of DVDs."

"Yes, I made two sets of DVDs. If you hadn't gotten this one you'd be watching me nag you about helping Ryland."

"Always thinking, Sab." Jennalyn lowered the stone from her lips. Her fingers continued rolling it around in her palm. The smooth surface absorbed her warmth. It did nothing to ease the pressure building in her chest. That she'd gotten used to seeing Sabrina's face on her TV—because she'd watched the last DVD over and over again in a desperate need to feel close to her baby sister—didn't ease the pressure.

"I know the project can't be easy for you, but I hope you're finding a little enjoyment planning the outings."

"I am."

"Do me another favor."

"Yes, puppet master."

"Tell Chrissy not to let you work too hard. And don't lock hope too deep inside. Be brave."

The screen went blank, leaving Jennalyn hungering for more. She watched it again and knew why she hadn't gotten more. It had been recorded on one of Sabrina's worst days. She barely stayed coherent for five minutes at a time. Jennalyn wasn't sure what hurt more...the message or the memory.

Chapter Seven

"It's colder than the ice king's—"

"What do you think of this one?" Ryland asked, interrupting Jennalyn. As much as he'd have enjoyed hearing her fill in the blank he wasn't so sure the mom shopping with her young daughter would feel the same.

Jennalyn scowled as she circled the tree. "It's a good one for the hospital location. The one for the main house should be bigger."

The woman's need for perfection was by turns admirable and annoying. Admirable in that he loved how much she wanted people to find some joy in an otherwise tough time. Annoying in that they'd walked the lot twice and Jennalyn still hadn't deemed a tree to be perfect enough for the main Ronald McDonald House.

"Bigger as in taller? Or bigger as in fatter?"

"Bigger." She curled her lip at him as if he were dense or even ignorant. "How hard is it to understand? The tree needs to be bigger."

He looked at her for a moment, trying to figure out why she was so surly. All day she'd been impatient and indecisive. It was as if she'd divorced herself for the day. Until he figured out what was rubbing her wrong he would be careful to modulate his voice.

"Do you want to walk the lot again? Or should we try another one?"

"Just pick a tree and let's be done with this. Looking more isn't going to help." She shrugged. "I'm not sure why I think I can find perfection. Especially today."

Especially today.

Like a two-ton baton, her words smacked him upside the head. Today was the anniversary of Sabrina's death. She had every right to be in a bad mood. Hell, he was impressed she was out of her house.

Signaling to the lot attendant that he wanted the tree she'd okayed, Ryland took Jennalyn's hand and pulled her to the benches surrounding the hot chocolate stand. It was still early enough in the month that the tree lot wasn't busy during a weekday. Still, Ryland picked the table farthest from the cocoa stand.

Leaving Jennalyn, he went for two drinks. She appeared, outwardly anyway, to be completely fine in her bubble of silence. He knew the pain of losing someone special, though. He recognized her outer shell as a façade. It was one he'd worn when he was eighteen.

Placing the paper cups on the table, Ryland slid onto the bench beside her. Several minutes passed in silence. They were minutes during which he hoped she would open up. Minutes during which he found his thoughts traveling back in time to his darkest moments. Moments that had set him on the path to becoming a doctor, which had led him to Jennalyn.

Life's domino effect was surreal.

"I know your pain, Jennalyn." He took her gloved hand in his and squeezed gently. "No amount of preparation or bracing makes this day any easier."

"You don't sound like a hospital professional offering a

platitude." She looked at him, really looked, for the first time all day. "You sound more like a man who's lost someone."

"You lost your sister who you were very close to. I lost a daughter I barely knew." *Elise.* Her name slid through his conscience, hushed by the distance of years. "There are no platitudes that cover lost love."

She looked up at him. Her brown eyes were dark. When she finally pushed words beyond the stranglehold of what he assumed to be suppressed tears, her voice was quiet and thick. "You've never mentioned a daughter."

"Only my family and a few close friends know about Elise. I was eighteen. She was unplanned, but damn I loved that kid."

"What happened to her?"

"SIDs." The world lodged in his throat. It always did, regardless of the circumstances because it always made him think of Elise's too-short life. "She was just under a year old."

Rather than offering words that would provide no comfort, she leaned against him. Her warmth soothed him, made him glad he'd decided to open up.

"How about her mother?"

The biggest mistake of my life. "I married her because it was the right thing to do."

Jennalyn tilted her head to glance at him for a moment. "That was a statement of fact with no emotion if ever there was one."

"As could be expected in those circumstances, Erin and I didn't last much past Elise's death. We barely worked even before that."

"A tune I know by heart. Sorry it didn't work for you."

He looked toward the trees, stared until they blurred. He never talked about Elise anymore, only replayed the same memories of snuggling her on his lowest days. She'd been the high point of his life. The best part of him. "I have her picture in my office so I never forget."

"Along with twenty other kids."

He shrugged. "Elise was the reason I became a pediatrician. I couldn't cure SIDs, but I could help other parents avoid the same loss."

"But you stopped practicing medicine."

"Actively. As an administrator I still impact lives. And it generally hurts a little less when we do lose a fight." For him, *we* was a collective term. When a patient didn't make it, the entire hospital felt it. His staff felt the losses on such a personal level that it was uncommon for at least one person not to attend each funeral.

"This month is a way of impacting lives."

"In a small way, yes."

"So explain the pictures in your office."

"Those are the patients I lost while I was actively practicing medicine." Their pictures were reminders of why he did his job. Each day, their smiling faces greeted him. Their spirits guided him.

The sad smile he had come to recognize as Jennalyn's normal smile stretched her lips. "You get better every time you open your mouth."

"You're not too shabby yourself, Jennalyn James." Going along with her change of mood, hoping it lasted the rest of the day, he released her hand to hug her close. "What do you say we go find a tree for the main house?"

She checked her watch and flinched. "Yes. We're going to have volunteers waiting on us if we don't."

They headed back to the lot to look at the trees once more.

Jennalyn's spirits, though still shadowed, were lighter. To keep things on the more casual footing, he hooked his arm around her waist as they walked. She settled against him, fitting as though she was his second half.

Not that he was going to say as much when she was raw from grief. Maybe, by the time the month was over, he'd see a miracle in Jennalyn. If he were really lucky, he would earn a small one for himself.

"If four out of five people suffer from diarrhea does that mean one enjoys it?"

Jennalyn's mouth twitched at the corner.

"Some people are like Slinkies."

Ryland continued his quest to cheer her up. His attempts had turned to bad jokes. Humoring him, she asked, "How?"

"They're not really good for anything, but you can't help smiling when you see one tumble down the stairs."

She chuckled. As much as she wanted to be glum, she couldn't stop herself. Ryland seemed to know that. He raised a brow and did a single head nod. It was like he was accepting a challenge and only he knew the rules.

"You ever play bridge, Jennalyn?"

"My parents did. Why?"

"I was just thinking about how sex is like playing bridge."

Yes. He was definitely the only one who knew the rules. There was no logic to his conversation path. She may not know the rules, but he had her wanting to smile if the tug in her cheeks was any indication.

"It scares me to ask, but how are bridge and sex alike?"

"If you don't have a good partner you better hope you have a good hand."

Jennalyn was still laughing a few minutes later when they pulled into the circular drive at Ronald McDonald House where Chrissy and Zack waited. Chrissy broke away from their intimate-looking chat and opened the passenger door.

"Are you okay?" Chrissy asked with a quizzical look.

"Fine." Jennalyn hopped out of the truck, looking forward to the rest of the day more than she'd thought possible.

"You're...laughing."

"Ryland has been telling jokes."

"You don't like jokes."

"Generally that's true."

But typical rules didn't apply to the medical professional in a cashmere sweater and leather coat who thought nothing of driving a beat-up truck or doing tasks he could easily pay for. The man who took the time to buy her cocoa, share his past and then tell her jokes.

Shaking her head, she watched Ryland unload the giant tree with Zack's help. "There's something about that man, Chrissy."

"So it would seem."

The unspoken humor in Chrissy's words blared like neon to Jennalyn. "What do you mean by that?"

"Nothing." Chrissy rolled her eyes—a signal that she was adjusting her stance. "Well, nothing if you being smitten can be considered nothing."

Jennalyn whipped around, stared at Chrissy. She spoke slowly to make sure she wasn't misunderstood. "I am not smitten. You on the other hand..." She wiggled a finger in Zack's general direction.

"That's too bad." Chrissy hooked her arm through Jennalyn's and led her inside. She ignored the dig about her and Zack, but her smile revealed the truth of what was going on. "Ryland is perfect for you."

"No man is perfect." They both looked back at the man lifting the trunk of the giant tree.

"Guess he'll just have to be perfect for someone else."

"Taunt all you want, Chrissy. I'm not in the market for a man."

"Then maybe you should take up bridge because you need something to do with yourself."

Jennalyn stumbled to a stop and stared at Chrissy's back as she kept walking. Her friend couldn't have known about Ryland's last joke. If she had known, Chrissy would have taken her remark much further. Still, it had Jennalyn thinking about playing bridge. Like any smart woman, though, she would wait for the right partner.

"Heavy tree coming through."

Ryland.

Jennalyn stepped aside and let Ryland and Zack pass. She'd helped load the tree, so she knew well how heavy the monstrosity was. The men made it look easy as they positioned it near the huge, brick fireplace. When they popped the strings holding the branches a collective gasp filled the room, coming from the mass of volunteers she'd barely noticed before.

Jennalyn smiled. At ten-feet tall and at least half that in diameter the tree they'd picked was impressive. After Chrissy introduced Jennalyn to all the volunteers—all fifty or so of them—and they were all settled back into the tasks they'd agreed to tackle, Jennalyn headed to the kitchen area for a drink. The tables had been covered with gauzy cloth that had snowflake patterns made with a silvery thread.

Each centerpiece was a clear glass cookie jar. Snowmen. Santas. Reindeer. They were all there and all with their bellies full of cookies of assorted shapes, sizes and Christmas-themed colors.

In the kitchen it looked like everyone had jumped aboard the Excess Express. She didn't see an inch of countertop that wasn't covered with casserole dishes, sandwich trays, fruit and veggie trays, and even more baked goods. Some of the baked goodies she recognized from the firehouse.

"The other kitchen here and the one at the hospital look just like this."

Jennalyn turned to see Zack leaning against a beam with his arms crossed and a smile brightening his handsome face. The green eyes that had laughed with everyone else over her ineptitude in the kitchen charmed her.

"Did you and the guys organize this?"

"A few of the guys with kids may have mentioned it to their wives who in turn mentioned it to the PTAs and booster clubs of their schools." He shrugged. "And none of your volunteers showed up empty-handed."

"There are a lot of volunteers." The list she'd gotten from Ryland had contained less than a third of the people who'd shown up. They had taken it upon themselves to invite their families, both immediate and extended.

"They have a lot to be grateful for. This is their way of saying thanks. And of making sure everyone staying here this year feels a little more at home."

The Christmas spirit echoed off the walls with the sounds of laughter and chatter, though on a more subdued level the reminder of such generosity was never absent from the House. Its evidence remained year-round in the form of a snow village that had been encased in a large glass box.

The village offered a message of hope that was as everlasting as the blue sky with fluffy clouds that had been painted on the ceiling of the main entrance. The ceiling was a gift a mother had donated to the House after her winter stay was finished. After months of going to the hospital too early in the morning and staying too late at night to ever see the sky, she'd wanted to do something for other parents. Her answer had been to hire a painter to turn the entryway ceiling into a replica of a light blue, cloud-filled sky that would allow other parents to always see the daytime sky.

Generosity became a living thing that breathed strength into everyone who volunteered at the Ronald McDonald House. Generosity and a loving desire to ease suffering in even the smallest ways.

Propelled by the beauty of that emotion, Jennalyn tracked down Chrissy, grabbed Zack and a couple of volunteers and headed to the company van outside.

The tree and decorating party had been Ryland's idea. Thanks to the help of Ronald McDonald House staff, Jennalyn had a surprise of her own.

Ryland used his foot to nudge the box of red bows along the floor before him. He was tying the bows to the evergreen garland that another volunteer was winding around the banister railing. The whole time he kept Jennalyn in his sights.

He continued to discover new levels to how much he enjoyed her company. There was a prideful thrill of victory when he made her smile or laugh, but being with her had turned into more. The promise to Sabrina no longer drove him. The outings for A Month of Miracles had become about more than rewarding a few special kids for their strength and bravery.

A Month of Miracles had turned into an escape, with each outing serving as another chance for him to see Jennalyn. Another chance to see her reveal a little more of herself, and what he saw made her more appealing.

Charisma. Kindness. Generosity.

She gave the best of herself to everyone and asked for nothing in return. Currently, unaware that she was being watched, Jennalyn gave her attention to Zack. Ryland wouldn't allow himself to speculate over the possible contents of their conversation. He didn't like what popped to mind. Frankly, he didn't like her talking to another man.

Possessive? Perhaps.

He wasn't accustomed to feeling jealous. Even as a teen, when he'd first started dating Erin, he'd never felt this way. He wanted to be the only man Jennalyn wanted to be with. Wanted to be the only one who could draw that serene smile to her lips. Or the glint of mischief that had flashed before she grabbed Chrissy, Zack and a few other volunteers to head outside.

They weren't gone long when she returned. She and each volunteer carried a box sporting the logo of a local glass blower.

Like the clichéd curious cat, Ryland abandoned his task and went to investigate, meeting Jennalyn and her helpers at the dining tables as she and Chrissy maneuvered the volunteers to stand by particular boxes. The commotion drew the attention of the others and within minutes everyone had grouped themselves by family.

Jennalyn moved to a box that sat alone. She ran her fingers along the edges. They shook lightly, yet she appeared in control.

Instinct had Ryland stepping up behind her, ready to give whatever support she may need.

"You all know that today was Ryland's idea." A quiver of a

tremble vibrated in Jennalyn's voice, but an inner strength kept her from cracking. "You are also familiar with, or will soon be, the miracles he's granting to a few special kids."

Everyone nodded. No one spoke.

"His generosity inspired me." She nodded toward the boxes. "The boxes before you are filled with hand-blown ornaments in two styles."

Each volunteer who'd carried a box in lifted off the lids. Their movements and reactions were almost identical and in the same order.

Gasps covered by hands over their mouths. Hands dropped to the ornaments tenderly. Brilliant smiles with a tear or two.

It wasn't until Jennalyn lifted her lid that Ryland understood. Nestled in the box, with probably three layers deep of nine ornaments, were fragile angel ornaments. They either floated with their wings outstretched or they walked on a brick-paved road with their wings tucked at their backs.

In a fine silver script that flowed as smoothly as a silken ribbon, a child's name graced each angel.

"The names represent children whose families stayed here at Ronald McDonald House. The earthbound angels are the ones who have overcome their illnesses and injuries thanks to Riley." Her voice dropped an octave as her left ring finger outlined the wings of the floating angel in the center of the box.

Sabrina's angel.

"The flying angels are those who now watch over us from above."

There were several of each design, but only one person in the room lifted a flying angel from their box. That was Jennalyn as she lifted Sabrina's angel.

As soon as she began planning this surprise, she had

known the reveal would come on the anniversary of Sabrina's death. Knowing, having time to prepare, wouldn't have done anything to ease the hurt. It was the same hurt he'd felt when talking about Elise. The same hurt he'd felt when he sat with Jennalyn at Sabrina's end. He'd cared for the little girl whose spirit had touched his. Maybe as much as Jennalyn had.

Ryland rested a hand on Jennalyn's shoulder and didn't try to stop the tears that fell from his eyes. Her breath shuddered as she hugged Sabrina's angel to her chest and turned into his arms.

Chapter Eight

Wrapped in the warmth of her Christmas robe and the fading glow of a satisfying day, Jennalyn picked up the glasses of wine she'd poured and returned to the living room. Ryland sat in the corner of the sofa she habitually curled up in. He had to know from the placement of the throw blanket, remote, book and coaster where she sat. Instead of asking if he'd intentionally taken her spot, she handed him a glass and moved to sit at the other end of the couch.

Silently, he captured her hand and pulled her to the cushion beside him. She'd settled with a shrug before he finally spoke.

"I hope you like action movies."

Leaning forward to place her wineglass on the table, her gaze landed on the bowl of rocks she'd placed his other gifts in. Mixed in with the larger rocks and stones were a bunch of little ones. They were all shiny with different shapes and colors. She picked up an aqua blue one and rubbed it between her fingers.

"When did you add these?"

"While you were changing."

"Do these have any special meaning?"

"They're pretty." He shrugged, as he so often seemed to do. "They started out as a rough material, but adversity shaped them into something even more beautiful. You're a little like them."

"You saying I started out rough?"

"I'm saying adversity makes us stronger. You're getting stronger every day." He kissed her temple and leaned back into the corner of the couch. "Now, do you like action movies?"

"They're okay." *Love them.*

He lifted the DVD remote and pressed play. "Then you'll have to suffer through *Captain America* for the sake of humoring me."

"Big words from the interloper who invited himself over for a movie."

The Marvel cartoon-esque pages flicked across the large screen. Ryland returned the remote to the table, set his wineglass down. Her question about what he was doing died in her throat as he wrapped his arms around her and pulled her close. He pressed his lips to her temple.

"The movie, while great, is second string to your company."

"You're just being nice because of what today is."

"Yeah. That's it. I don't really enjoy your company."

Intellectually she knew he was kidding. He was too kind to speak so abruptly even if it was true. Intellectual insight couldn't be seen when the glare of emotional wounds kicked up.

Kris had been sweet in the beginning. Like Ryland. He'd used sarcasm as humor. Until it had become a truth. He'd been packing his bags the last time he'd spoken to her. That he didn't enjoy her company had been the nicest thing he'd said.

On TV, a scrawny kid was getting beat up in an alley. For Jennalyn, each punch landed with the knuckle smack of pain. Each fist was a striking memory leaving a fresh mark. Then the would-be hero was rescued from his hell.

A year had passed since Kris walked out.

A year had passed since Sabrina passed.

A year had passed before a hero came to rescue Jennalyn from her hell.

Ryland.

Settling deeper into his warmth, she drew on the closeness of his compassion. He'd listened to her, talked with her, joked with her. Now, ignoring her arguments that she was fine, he'd stayed with her.

Her cheek rested on Ryland's chest. The softness of his sweater was a caress as tender as his fingers moving rhythmically over her arm. Tears lodged in her throat. The TV blurred until she no longer saw the movie. Then shapes blurred into colors that faded.

On a level clouded with dreams and swelling music, she floated weightless and secure. Then she was no longer drifting and a feather touch brushed her forehead. Awareness dawned slowly.

She was in her bed. She'd fallen asleep. Ryland had tucked her in.

She could still feel his sweater beneath her cheek and smell the scent of pine tree on him. She still sensed his strength. Half afraid to find him gone, hoping she wouldn't, Jennalyn opened her eyes. Ryland sat at the edge of her bed watching her.

"You're still here?" It was a ridiculous question, sort of like calling someone at home to ask if they're home. It was obvious, but also the only thing that popped into her mind.

"I couldn't leave you alone."

"Why?"

His eyes never left hers. "Didn't want to."

"How long ago did…"

He shrugged and kept watching her. Instead of feeling awkward she somehow felt right with him watching over her. And that was a strange idea because she'd never been the kind to accept emotional support. She always gave it.

It had been one of the things Kris had twisted, saying she was cold and impossible to get close to. She was realizing the biggest reason for her broken engagement had not been because of her. For the first time she was genuinely happy that Kris had walked.

Having left the week before Sabrina died, his timing had sucked. He'd handled it badly and resorted to unkindness. The when and how no longer mattered because he had done her a favor. The favor she'd been given by Ryland though, the generosity of himself, showed her the depth of a real man.

"I should go." Ryland's words pulled her from the quagmire of her thoughts.

"Why?"

"Because if I stay I'll want to kiss you."

"Okay."

"I shouldn't kiss you tonight."

"Why?"

"Kissing you," he continued as if she didn't speak, "while you're in bed would be too strong a temptation."

"I'm okay with temptation." The distraction from life promised to be pleasurable. Surely they couldn't regret pleasure.

"You're vulnerable." His hand moved from his thigh to hers. "Feeling lonely."

"Vulnerable. Maybe."

"Definitely."

It was her turn to shrug because she couldn't dispute her vulnerability. "I may even be lonely but that doesn't mean I have to be alone."

"Jennalyn." He leaned down, tightening the grip on her thigh. His lips pressed against hers, setting her belly to fluttering. Just when she thought he'd lower more, melt into the pleasure, he pulled away.

Her hand covered his on her thigh. "I'm not sure why I'm going to admit this."

"What?"

"Your company was exactly what I needed tonight." Pressure squeezed her hand and moved up her arm to her heart. Her chest shrank. "You've made this day bearable when I was dreading it."

His gaze had held hers since she'd opened her eyes. Now he dropped it to their joined hands. A sigh shook his chest.

"You weaken a man's will."

Her heart hammered her ribs, haunted her with the fear that he'd walk out. "You weaken a woman's."

"I'll stay with you. I'll hold you." He pulled the cover back and lay beside her fully clothed.

"You're a noble man, Ryland Davids." She snuggled into his arms, wondering if in the light of morning she'd regret her vulnerability.

Two steps into the Indianapolis Children's Museum was all it took to have Diamond, shortened affectionately to Di, bouncing. And to have Ryland, Jennalyn and Di's mom Ashley laughing. Though Ashley's laugh was a little tense.

"It's Bumblebee." Di's ringlet curls danced along her back. "I love Bumblebee. And holy cow, look at the dinosaurs coming through the wall. That big one is a brontosaurus."

The seven-year-old's voice cracked with a squeal about the dinosaurs even as she raced in circles around the Transformer that stood proud in the main lobby. After two laps she slowed down to keep pace with the turning base that kept the robot circling.

Jennalyn took everyone's coats. "I'll stow these in a locker and get our tickets." She handed Ryland her camera before moving to stand in line. "You handle the pictures."

Ashley relaxed a bit when she left. Her tension, though unnecessary, in regard to Jennalyn, was second nature. She was warming up though. "I can't believe you picked Di for today."

Ryland looked at Ashley, her height matching his to the inch. The woman who'd been seen as intimidating when she found her daughter injured had been beaten down by circumstances. Her trust was fragile; especially toward women she barely knew. Ryland hoped to help her overcome that just as he hoped to make the day special for Di.

"I explained it when I called," he said while taking pictures of Di. "Di suffered enough. She deserves a day of fun."

"You did." Her gaze darted to Jennalyn, who stood in the ticket line, while Di chatted up a museum employee near Bumblebee. Ashley, always wary of adults she didn't know, moved a little closer. "And though you know how appreciative I am I can't help feeling hesitant."

"Which is why you're with us. Nothing bad is going to happen to your angel today."

Di had lain in a hospital bed covered with third- and fourth-degree burns. In the grips of agony, she had worried more about the feelings of her mom and dad than her own comfort. The jovial child with kindness in her core wouldn't experience so much as the sting of a *no* on his watch.

"Thank you, Ryland." Ashley's shoulders stiffened.

With his back turned and even without the shift in Ashley's posture, Ryland felt a vibration move the air around him. Jennalyn was back. He'd never bought into the whoo whoo kind of stuff, but the only way he could explain it to himself was that it felt like his aura shifted to make room for her. It was equally creepy and exciting.

"Are we ready?" Jennalyn rested her fingers on his arm. Only the tips for the briefest moment. It was enough.

His breath caught. His pulse jumped.

The restraint he found to behave civilly, to not drag her into a corner of the nearby hall amazed him. It had been the same way every time she'd touched him since waking in his arms that morning. Fully clothed and with the barrier of her ridiculously cute and fluffy robe, he'd been struck by the simplicity of being with her. She was a complex woman full of grief and layers of intrigue, but being in her company made perfect sense.

"I'm more than ready." Eager for more of her, he took Jennalyn's hand and linked their fingers.

Ashley took Di's hand and together they went to hand over their tickets.

Jennalyn smiled at Di. "I hear you like science."

"Yes."

"Do you have a favorite science show you watch?"

"*Nova.*" Di's answer was high pitched and immediate. "My dad watches it. He recorded bunches for me when I was in the hospital."

"What was your favorite episode?"

Jennalyn shifted so she was walking beside Di. Her hand brushed the little girl's bangs from her forehead. Ashley stiffened. Ryland waited.

Jennalyn was either unaware of Ashley's discomfort, or she was ignoring it in an attempt to keep things low stress. If Ashley would open herself up to the possibility of trust she would see that the only thing Jennalyn had to offer was goodness.

"Well, the one on the twins who were joined at the brain was cool. And the one where they mine for elements. I think it would be fun to go mining. Oh, and there was one about tornadoes and another about mastodons like in *Ice Age*. I *really* like the ones about dinosaurs though."

Jennalyn didn't laugh or appear surprised at the rushed thoughts of a child. She followed along perfectly. "Do you think you would like to meet a paleontologist who used to be on *Nova?*"

"Oh my gosh. Yes! That would be so cool." Di's words raced over the top of each other.

"Then let's head this way." Jennalyn steered them toward the right. They rounded a corner and before them, suspended in flight, hung several pterodactyls.

Di grew more animated as she launched into a lecture about how the name meant winged finger, which she thought was pretty weird because it looked nothing like a finger. Before they could agree with her, she proceeded to tell them that the wingspan of the pterodactyl, which was really a flying reptile and not a dinosaur, could be over forty feet long.

"That's ten of me!"

"You didn't learn all of that from *Nova*, did you?" Ryland asked.

"Of course not." She chuckled as if he were truly silly. "I have books too."

98

"Books upon books upon books," Ashley joked. Wrapped up in the joy of her daughter, she'd loosened up enough to release her grip on Di. Her regard of Jennalyn had softened a tiny bit too.

"My sister, Sabrina, was the same way with books." Ryland hadn't heard Jennalyn talk about Sabrina without sadness. Until now. The only thing in her tone was pride and a fond memory.

"Di would read the *Encyclopedia Britannica* cover to cover if we had them."

"But we don't so I have to settle with what I can get." Di pulled the attention back to her as only a child could. "At least I have a computer at home. I can look stuff up on that."

Jennalyn and Di continued their discussion, with occasional additions from Ashley and Ryland, about dinosaurs and research sources as they made their way through the dinosaur exhibit. It took them close to an hour, with Di quizzing every museum employee she met. Finally they made it to the lab where a paleontologist worked on recreating a T-Rex skull.

Di started to race to the open window. Jennalyn stopped her plunge into questions with a quick hand on her shoulder. Ashley tensed, but the moment passed quickly.

Ashley followed with Ryland as Jennalyn spoke to the scientist. It was another sign of Ashley's growing trust that she hung back.

Whatever Jennalyn said had a smile splitting the paleontologist's previously dour face. Placing his paintbrush on the table, he motioned Jennalyn and Di over to the large glass doors. Just inside, he presented Di with a white lab coat that had her name embroidered over one pocket.

Ryland and Ashley moved to the lab. Ashley joined Di as the paleontologist gave her a tour and explained what all the tools were for. Jennalyn appeared at peace as she leaned against a counter to watch from a distance. An easy smile rested on her lips as she watched the science-loving little girl explore a dream come true.

"You continue to amaze me, JJ."

She shifted her gaze to him. Her smile slipped into a shadow that thankfully passed quickly. "Just doing the job."

"You do more than that." He leaned against the counter, bumping his shoulder to her. "You've made that girl's year."

"She deserves it."

"And you've shown her mother that it's okay to trust her child to other women."

Curiosity crinkled her brow into a tiny up and down line on her forehead. "Why wouldn't that be okay?"

"Because the last woman she allowed near Di without her supervision set her on fire." He kept his voice low, but volume control had no softening impact on such brutal words.

Jennalyn controlled her gasp, but the horror sat ripe in her eyes. Rage and sorrow also showed themselves.

"What the hell is wrong with people?" She turned her stare to Di, shook her head. "Maybe someone should have set *her* on fire. As if kids don't have a tough enough time. Why make it harder?"

"I second that thought, even if I couldn't condone it. That's one of those life questions that will never be adequately answered." He slipped the camera into a pocket and wrapped an arm around her waist. Touching her casually became easier all the time. After she'd trusted him with the honor of holding her in a moment of vulnerability it felt like something he'd been born for.

"Every experience leads us down a new path." His

experiences had led to her. "Di suffered agonizing pain, both from her burns and skin grafts, but maybe the joy of today makes it worthwhile."

"*Nothing* can make that kind of abuse worthwhile."

"Why not? Because of that abuse Di has already seen beauty in its purest form. She's seen the truest meaning of a giving spirit thanks to a donor. And thanks to you for setting up this tour." For all they knew Jennalyn had just set a little girl onto a path that would lead to an amazing and fulfilling career.

Chapter Nine

Jennalyn pulled her legs up under her and wrapped the thick robe around her legs. It was a little cold to be outside, but being inside felt a too stifling. Cocoa steam rose from her mug as she sat in a padded chaise on her front porch. Beyond the covered perch, thick and fluffy flakes of snow tumbled to the ground, covering it with a thick blanket of perfection she always appreciated. A crisp, fresh aroma that came only with a new snow filled the air.

It had snowed the night Sabrina passed away. Deep inside, so deep she hadn't been able to pinpoint the thought, Jennalyn played with the idea that the snow was Sabrina's way of saying she was in a better place. Only God and angels could create such perfection and Sabrina had definitely been an angel.

Her DVD messages hurt. They tore at Jennalyn's heart even as she craved the next one. Every one reminded her that the best way to honor Sabrina and their parents was to start fresh. Her heart had been broken, but it had been time to pick up the pieces. It was a lesson she'd been hesitant to accept, but she'd been doing that with Ryland and A Month of Miracles. She found herself looking forward to each outing more than the last.

She even found herself anticipating the small gifts Ryland left her with. Her hand slid into her pocket and her mind drifted back to them standing in the museum gift shop.

Ryland placed a large pink rock—a rose quartz—into her palm.

"You keep giving me rocks. Why?"

"You collect them."

"Sabrina did."

"But you encouraged her. You helped her find new ones, and you always knew their meaning."

"So you're trying to keep that memory alive?"

"That." He pressed the pink stone into her hand. "And they're pretty. Like you."

"You said that before." The smile couldn't have been held back if she'd wanted it to be. Not that she could've thought of a reason not to smile. The other times he'd given her a rock he'd had an explanation on why he'd chosen it. Curiosity called for one now.

She was sure he'd say he'd have to look it up, so she asked, "Do you know what makes this stone special?"

"It's the love gemstone. The love you had for your family, for Sabrina, and the love you gift these kids with is transcendental."

She rolled her eyes in her mind, but she wanted what he said to be true. She wanted him to really see her that way, because it sounded simply wonderful.

"It also brings optimism and healing, sometimes happiness."

"As a medical professional you're giving a rock credit for healing people?"

"Not all wounds are medical in nature. The rose quartz helps balance emotions and can spark the energy to heal broken hearts."

Rubbing the small rock hours later, as Ryland's words

103

replayed in her memory, she again though the sentiment a lovely one. On the off chance the quartz really could ease her heart, she slipped it back into her pocket. It would also be in her purse or pocket for the foreseeable future.

"You're going to freeze out here."

"Ryland." Jennalyn turned in her chair to see Ryland watching her with his hands buried in his jacket pockets. His nose and the tips of his ears were pink. Propped against the house by the front door was a Christmas tree.

"You brought me a tree?"

"I noticed you hadn't gotten around to getting yourself one."

"It's just me. What's the point?"

"You enjoy them. You need no other point."

He didn't tell her it wasn't just her, or say that he'd be around. He gave her no promise of such words and she wanted them. Wanting them scared her because she didn't do emotion well these days. Shutting down the desire, she asked, "What makes you think I enjoy them?"

"Because I watched you shop the lot. Then I watched you decorate to the last strand of perfectly placed tinsel."

"A tree without presents beneath it is a sad tree. I have no presents."

"It's sadder still to have no tree." He held a hand out. "Now, are you going to come decorate it or are you going to continue being a masochist?"

"A masochist?" That's one she'd never been accused of being before.

"When it comes to your skill at denying yourself, at living in your grief, there's no better term for you."

"Don't sugarcoat your opinions there, Ryland."

"Doing so would waste my time and do you no favors."

The tone of his words suggested the favors he spoke of were something only he could give. "What exactly do you think your favors are doing for me?"

"Getting you out of your grief-filled rut."

She stood, stalked to him in her robe and slipper-encased feet. "As if it's your job to fix me. Who do you think you are?"

"I'm the man who hired you to plan several events. Who's trying to make you see how much stronger you can be."

"And we don't have another one planned for two days." She walked around him, seething internally that she'd allowed herself to think they'd become more than business acquaintances. She'd respected him because he hadn't flaunted his position. He hadn't made it out like he was the better of the two of them. He hadn't acted like Kris. Until now.

"I don't need your kind of favors." She opened the door, gripped the knob until her knuckles hurt. "You know nothing about me. Take your tree and go save someone else."

"Jennalyn."

Shaking her head, not interested in anything more he had to say, she went inside and shut the door. Her chest ached. She didn't like fights any more than she liked to know she'd misread Ryland. Expecting him to knock or try to plead his case, she watched through the peephole.

He stood outside, looking like he'd been kicked. His mouth opened and closed as he tried to formulate words or decide his next move. Then his shoulders sank, he ducked his head and walked away.

He left the tree.

It was still snowing two days later when Jennalyn made her

way from a parking garage to the hospital's main entrance. Her blood heated with every step that took her closer, but it was too cold to remove her scarf or unbutton her coat. A few flakes slid beneath her scarf. The hint of cold was short-lived before her heated body melted them. Those few moments made breathing easier.

Her anxiety hadn't eased over her last visits to the hospital. The day they'd decorated the tree in Ronald McDonald House in the hospital, after wrapping up at the main house, had almost shattered her last barrier.

It had been a long day for her, but everyone involved had seemed to enjoy it. The families coming in for food or an escape had appreciated the work. Jennalyn had been swamped with memories, and she hadn't been able to stop herself from looking at every red wagon she'd seen.

She hadn't seen the one she sponsored in Sabrina's name and the blend of crushing disappointment and irrational relief began a new battle in the chambers of her heart as she approached the front doors. Crossing the threshold into electric warmth, Jennalyn scanned the lobby, half looking for red wagons. She saw one near the fountain. Her heart rose a beat.

She saw the generic license plate on the back. Her heart sank back into its regular rhythm.

"Jennalyn," a perky voice, feminine to its saccharin core, interrupted her mental morass. "It's so great to see you."

Friendly arms encircled her before she could compute what was happening, and almost before she recognized Rhea. The woman had been Sabrina's day nurse and as well as they'd gotten to know each other, Jennalyn still stiffened in the embrace.

The nurse's touch stung like the prick of an incorrectly placed IV needle. She patted Rhea's back. Once. Twice.

Be nice and she'll go to work quickly. "It's great to see you."

Rhea, always undeterred by someone's desire for space, squeezed her tighter. The sting penetrated more deeply. Almost to the bone. Blissfully unaware of the discomfort she caused, she released Jennalyn.

"I've been hoping you would come back."

"I've been busy."

"Everyone is talking about A Month of Miracles. About a few of the things you and Ryland have done so far."

"Speaking of Ryland." Jennalyn stepped with one foot in the direction of Ryland's office. The hint failed to register along the tangling pathways of Rhea's brain.

"You're here for the concert today, aren't you?"

"Yes." A step toward Ryland's offices and still Rhea continued.

"The kids are really looking forward to it. They're so eager to see who the surprise guests are."

"The wait is almost over." Jennalyn took two more steps toward Ryland's office with Rhea still following.

"It's driving them crazy. Has them all playing guessing games."

"Anticipation is half the fun." Jennalyn put her hand on Rhea's arm before the chattering busybody could go on. "Before we can get set up and started I need to talk to Ryland."

She had to apologize for her behavior. For being so shut off she'd gotten defensive when he'd only been being kind.

"You two are great together." The woman, old enough to be Jennalyn's mother, patted her hand. "You go talk to your man."

Jennalyn almost ignored the last statement. If she'd thought for a moment Rhea wouldn't go gossip with more of Ryland's staff she'd have let it go. Professionalism was too big a deal to her though. "He isn't my man."

"You're getting very close."

"We're working together. When the month is over our time together will end." Each word became a domino tumbling emotion after emotion. Tumbling with emotions she couldn't separate came two truths. She meant what she said. Yet, she didn't want them to be the truth.

Ryland wasn't in his office when she finally broke away from Rhea. She left a message with his admin that she'd like to speak to him and then she went to oversee the setup for the concert.

Despite the weather they'd decided to hold the gathering in the courtyard outside the library. In the early days of the hospital it had been a circular drive. Now it was a large courtyard surrounded by the building. As a concession to the cold they'd brought in a tent and several heaters to keep everyone warm. Stepping through the flaps, Jennalyn was pleased at the warmth waiting. Patients would need no more than a light robe to stay warm.

The stage had been set at one end with large speakers on either side. A platform had been placed in the middle where a camera sat. They would do a live stream of the concert into the patient rooms so the kids who couldn't come down could still see the concert. To make everyone comfortable while making sure they could see, risers of varying heights had been brought in. A ramp led to each one for wagons and wheelchairs and there would be plenty of chairs, so no one stood.

In the middle of the space was a throne-like chair where a professional Santa would sit. After the concert he would stay until he'd talked with every child.

At one end of the tent was a stage. Behind the stage was another section of tent that would hide the guests until the right moment. The only guest who would be kept separate was the child receiving today's miracle.

Things were in great shape, but there were still AV checks to be done, as well as other last-minute confirmations. Then the special guests would arrive and with them a host of other chores she'd lined up volunteers for. Several hours had passed. Ryland stayed too busy wherever he was to come see her. The longer she waited the higher her blood pressure rose. She hadn't decided what she would say to him, but she knew she had to apologize. The longer she waited the more her hateful words burned.

Her phone rang. It was Ryland's office. She swallowed, choking down the bitter taste of crow she hadn't eaten yet. "Hello."

"Jennalyn, it's Blanche." Ryland's grandmotherly assistant.

"Yes, Blanche."

"Your guests have arrived. Mr. Davids will be coming down with them in a few minutes."

"Excellent. Thank you." *He* couldn't call to tell her that? By the time she got to see him they'd be surrounded by guests and patients. The time to talk would be gone. Disappointment was a masked phantom behind the haze of mounting frustration. The man was making an apology impossible.

As she was hanging up, the tent flaps opened. Two men stepped in, dressed as toy soldiers. They held the flaps open for four elves and Santa. Plastering on a smile she didn't feel, Jennalyn greeted the newcomers and led them to their seats.

She no sooner had the Christmas crew settled when the flaps were again opened by the soldiers. Filing in, a little timidly though clearly excited, were the first of the patients. She worked with the nurses to get everyone in and seated. The whole time her gaze sought Ryland.

He should be down with the guests, but he'd stayed out of sight. The longer she was in the hospital without seeing him the more her irritation grew. She'd missed him. She hadn't missed any man ever, but she missed Ryland.

She checked her watch, impatient for the time to pass so she could have a few moments alone with Ryland. They were supposed to begin in just a few minutes, so he had to be in the holding room with their guests. Patients, staff and too little time stretched the distance. Edging around the crowd, Jennalyn made it less than halfway to the stage before their MC for the concert entered from the back flaps of the tent. Ryland's gaze met hers through the opening. In the instant before the flaps fell back into place a chill more intense than the freezing temperatures outside blasted her.

She needed to come up with an amazing apology.

Whatever the MC said that got the crowd laughing and then cheering was lost on her. Her own anticipation at seeing select members of the *Glee* cast failed to penetrate. A corner of her brain registered that Kurt was on the stage, and another part registered that he sang his rendition of "Blackbird".

Jennalyn had anticipated the moment, but even the pure beauty of his voice failed to touch her as it so often did. Kurt—Chris Colfer—wrapped up. The applause swelled and then subsided. More cast members came out and sang more songs. Each time the kids cheered. Each time Jennalyn wished it was the last because each carol lost more cheer with her desire to speak with Ryland.

The MC returned to introduce the next song. The *Glee* members stepped aside as his words penetrated a little more deeply than before.

"Some of you know our next guest since she's been a patient here. I've been told stories about how she would walk through the halls singing."

Jennalyn's head rose a little higher.

"Her favorite song was 'Brave' by Idina Menzel."

Tears puddled along Jennalyn's lower lid. She'd heard a girl walking the halls and singing on several occasions. A quiet power had carried the impactful lyrics beyond doors closed for privacy. Even beyond the wretched wails of loss.

"A girl who stayed brave in the face of a kidney disease that almost killed her is here to sing for us today. Help me welcome Rachel Saltzman to our stage."

The MC stepped back as a young girl, maybe fourteen, came into the tent. Her skin looked impossibly pale against her midnight hair, but a healthy blush hued her cheeks. Joy, and a wisdom beyond her years, gave her gaze an eerie punch.

Rachel.

Jennalyn hadn't realized the girl on her list who liked to sing was the same girl she'd heard in the halls. The girl who'd walked the halls while Jennalyn had waited for Sabrina to draw her last breath. She'd never seen the girl, but the sweet voice had come back to her often.

"Rachel was lucky enough to receive a new kidney, and she's doing great. And just as her singing in the halls reminded patients, family and staff that every life—however brief—is a blessing, your presence today tells us the same."

The puddles of tears at Jennalyn's lower lids deepened.

The MC handed Rachel a microphone and thanked her for joining them.

"Thank you." Her sweet voice had matured with a strength that rang with hope as she spoke. "Riley and the friends I found here gave me the courage to fight my illness."

"Did you ever think you wouldn't get better?"

"How could I not when I spent more time in the hospital that I did at home?" Rachel looked at the kids in the room in a way that could make every one of them believe she addressed them directly. "No matter how tough the roughest day was, no matter how overwhelmed I became, I couldn't let despair rule. The second I gave in to it was the second I lost."

"It's important to fight."

"To our last breath, whenever it comes."

Freely, like a river swollen from a heavy rain, the tears flowed from Jennalyn's eyes. The girl's maturity awed her. Knowing what would come next for the girl was just as awesome.

"To celebrate that fight for life we have a surprise for you, Rachel."

At the back of the stage, Ryland opened the tent flaps. The *Glee* cast members on stage applauded. Rachel turned. She gasped. Then giggled.

Standing in the opening was Idina Menzel, the original singer of Rachel's anthem. The woman who commanded a Broadway stage, the big screen and small screen with equal aplomb moved to Rachel. With a wide smile, she embraced the girl.

Together, sitting on stools side-by-side, they turned "Brave" into a stunning duet. Neither held back as they sang about being brave even when life was daunting. They reminded Jennalyn of Sabrina's request that she be brave.

Being brave meant more than going to work each day.

Refusing to wait for a perfect moment, Jennalyn left the tent and circled back to the smaller section were Ryland was.

He turned, looking striking and powerful as he had the night at the zoo. The words she wanted still evaded her. She could only raise her hands before her and whisper, "I'm sorry."

Ryland came to her, as he had that night, and stood before her. Gazes locked. "Never apologize to me for your feelings."

"I was rude."

"You were hurting." He brushed a tear from her cheek. "Sorry I've been too busy to see you before now today."

"Make it up to me."

"How?"

She smiled, felt it in her heart. He made being brave easy. "Help me decorate my tree."

Chapter Ten

Pine, cinnamon and cocoa scented her living room. A guitar, lovingly strummed and backed up with other stringed instruments, accompanied a gorgeous version of "No Day But Today". It was a divorce from the traditional Christmas songs that had been playing, but it suited the mood as Jennalyn stepped back from hanging the last ornament on the tree.

Ryland flipped the wall switch, casting the living room in a soft white glow. Returning to Jennalyn, he wrapped his arms around her. With her back to his chest they inspected their work.

"I had you pegged as a colored lights kind of girl."

She allowed her head to rest against his shoulder. A deep sigh slipped free, but it didn't feel sad. He viewed it as a positive sign.

"People always said that when I decorated my tree. Most of them then argued that clear lights are cold. As if they think of me as cold."

"There's nothing cold about a Christmas tree. Or you."

"Then where does the expectation come from?"

"From your passion. The clear reflects your love of organization."

She snorted. Not a laugh. No, it was a full snort. "Until

Chrissy got her hands on me I was the most unorganized person you could've known."

"No way."

"Oh yeah. I'll prove it." She pulled free of his arms and motioned for him to follow.

He raised a brow, but didn't argue as he followed her to her bedroom. "An unmade bed doesn't count."

She shook her head and headed up the stairs. "If only that was the worst of it."

"Are you going to show me your skeletons?"

"There could be a few of those too." She crossed her room and grasped the handles of the double closet doors. A silent dare, her gaze met his over her shoulder. "If you've a weak constitution..."

"It can't be that bad."

"I haven't allowed Chrissy to see this. She'd have a stroke." With a shrug, she tugged on the doors.

The closet was nearly as big as her room, which was a pretty good size. Hangers filled every row. Some held clothes. Some didn't. All of them were stuffed so tightly they didn't actually fit. Shoes were jammed two and three layers deep onto shelves until they spilled off and onto the floor. The floor was a whole other situation. What looked like three piles of clothes had bled into one larger one. Neatly hanging on two door hooks was her "I Believe in Santa" robe. Sabrina's was on a hook beside it.

Ryland looked back at Jennalyn. She stood with her chin high, her shoulders back. Her outfit was perfectly coordinated and wrinkle free.

"How long does it take you to get dressed in the morning?"

"Not as long as it takes to find the clothes. And then iron

them."

The lady was an organized shell with a messy center. That she put herself through a crazy routine every morning when she knew the value of organization made her more endearing. It was an imperfection he liked.

"You are shattering my illusions, JJ." He'd only called her JJ twice, but somehow it seemed to suit the moment.

"What illusions?"

"That you're perfect." Three short strides carried him to her. "You're always so put together on the outside." He traced the pressed seam of her sleeve. "Professional." He fidgeted with the edge of her sleeve, tugging lightly. "Organized." His gaze engaged hers. Held her prisoner. "In control."

"Not always."

"Says the woman who continually gives her all to others while never asking for her own comfort."

"I've just been doing my job."

"Tremendously. But there's more to it than that." He had gotten emails from everyone they'd dealt with so far, each one praising the initiative. The joy that Jennalyn's plans started was rippling into the community with regular people taking it upon themselves to perform miracles.

She'd mistaken his thoughts when their eyes had met at the concert. Yes, he'd been angry, but it had been aimed at himself. He'd assumed she would enjoy a tree, especially after watching her at the Ronald McDonald House. It had been part of the mask she seemed never to be without. It was the same mask that was revealed only by the opening of her closet. She was as messy on an emotional level as her closet was. Messy might be too mild a description. Chaos was a better fit.

He wanted her to see that he understood her. He valued the

trust she'd placed in him. He cared enough not to push too far too fast.

"I'm growing to admire you more and more."

"Ryland—"

He sealed whatever argument she might have behind her lips. With his. He didn't step closer. He didn't grab her beyond flattening his hand on her bicep. He didn't move his lips against hers.

The kiss was a touch of lips in a quiet break from the world. It was nothing more. And so much more.

The touch of lips sparked a flame that spread through him. Blood. Bone. Muscle. Marrow. Every cell was touched.

The quiet break from the world became a breath that hummed around them. Silken. Sweet. Tingling. Testing. Every breath was broken.

His lids slid closed. His mind catalogued each impression. It was like he was dancing along a slick surface with the perfect partner. Then she leaned in, pressing her lips more fully to his.

Warmth became chills that raised the hair follicles on his arms. The moment suspended in perfection, as if the earth had stopped its rotation.

Her lips flexed. It was a tiny movement, one he felt to the depths of his tightening gut. Their energies danced. Weightless, he was poised at the edge of serenity. If he had wings, or a sprinkle of pixie dust, he would take flight. There was no happier moment than this one with Jennalyn close enough to breathe in.

He backed away, but only his lips and only for the sake of resting his forehead against hers. "You're a tempting woman, JJ."

She hooked a nail on one of his shirt buttons and tugged

lightly. "How tempting?"

"Very."

"Then stay. Sleep with me."

His arms grew heavy with the desire to pull her close. He'd held her through the night once. The impression of her curves hugged against him was inescapable. Not that he wanted escape.

"That's not a good idea."

"Because of work?" Defensiveness crept into her tone. It had been the same the night he delivered her tree. Wiser than an average dumbass incapable of learning a lesson, he knew where the tone came from. And where it could lead.

"Because when I lie down with you again it isn't going to be to hold you while you're down."

"I'm not down."

"Neither is it going to be at the end of a day that's ripped you apart inside."

"Then you'll never lie with me, because every day without my family rips at me."

He shook his head. "You'll experience a truly great day again."

"There are no good days. Certainly great ones don't exist."

He would prove her wrong, but not with a verbal sparring match. Keeping them both on their feet would be much more fun. More rewarding.

With another brief kiss, he took the hand she had on his shirt and pressed a stone into it. She pulled back with a moaning sigh and looked quizzically at the amethyst cluster.

"I have one of these."

"Did you know they're good for keeping the air and life force of your home clean and positive?"

"I did."

"Then you know that feeds directly into its calming properties." He kissed her again. "Put it under your pillow and have pleasant dreams."

"You're an unexpected man."

"Expected is dull." After a final kiss, one he lingered a little longer over, Ryland left. The last few days without Jennalyn had been lackluster to the point of lifelessness. He was finished living with lackluster.

Jennalyn sat on a bench beside the ice and watched the skaters as they sailed along the shiny surface. Grace and elegance flowed behind them, laughed on the breeze like their flapping scarves of vibrant Christmas colors. Red and green, silver and blue, yellow and gold. They were all present from the poinsettias in their gift-wrapped pots circling the ice to the ice sculpture center rink that depicted a snow globe.

Straight No Chaser's "Twelve Days of Christmas" jingled through the mall's speaker system enhancing the feel of the season.

"Ready?" Ryland asked from beside her. He wasn't talking to her though.

"Yes." Dawn, a nine-year-old who'd recently received a clean bill of health thanks to a new pancreas, did a little bounce on the thin blades of her skates. "I've missed the ice."

"Then let's go." Ryland tugged on the thin scarf she'd wrapped around her throat. "You promised to teach me a jump."

Jennalyn waved her cell and winked at Dawn. "I'm ready to

dial 9-1-1 so don't worry too much about him getting hurt."

"He'll be okay."

"Yes, he will," Ryland put in.

"Hopefully." Jennalyn patted his arm just above his hand. "But face the facts. You may be as good once as you ever were, but only once."

"I'll show you how good I am."

"I'm ready to be underwhelmed."

Dawn laughed and headed toward the ice. Ryland abandoned the sparring match and followed her. For the next hour, Jennalyn took pictures of Dawn and Ryland. Dawn had skated competitively before getting sick, and it turned out that Ryland didn't suck on the narrow strips of metal.

When Dawn gave him an instruction for a jump he obeyed. He landed on his ass more often than not, but he kept trying again. Laughing from the sidelines was fine, because she had never been on skates and they terrified her, but the longer she watched Ryland and Dawn the more she realized where the real fun was.

On the ice.

Lacing up her brave pants, Jennalyn went after a pair of skates and teetered her way across the rubber floor.

"I live in heels. How is it so hard to walk in these?" she muttered as she stared at the ice. One step and she'd be on the slippery surface.

If she were lucky she would glide like most of the people. She doubted that she would be so lucky. No. She would feel the smack of her backside before it was all over. Probably before it fully began.

Courage is looking fear in the face and laughing or screaming as you do it anyway.

The advice had come from their dad any time she'd been hesitant to try something new. Though her mom always wanted her to work for their business her dad gave her the courage to break tradition. Without him she wouldn't have gone to school for business and marketing. She would have always wondered if she missed out on some great life experience.

Glide. Embrace the moment.

Her dad's voice was a quiet rumble that rose higher and turned louder into laughter on the ice beyond. His daring humor channeled through the people on the ice. It pulled at her. She lifted a foot and put it back down.

Large and open-palmed, a hand broke her line of vision. "I won't let you fall."

Ryland.

Glancing up into his earnest eyes, she placed her hand in his. The first step wasn't too bad. She just kept more weight on the foot that was planted on the rubber floor. The second step was the worst. In those few seconds when one foot sat on slick ground and the other moved through the air, doubt and fear leapt back in.

The song on the sound system changed from "Jingle Bells" to "Baby, It's Cold Outside". Ryland held her hands, skating backward as they moved around the outer edge of the ice. After a lap of being pulled in a gentle glide, she risked lifting one foot and then the other. After another lap, Jennalyn found her rhythm. Her shoulders bounced in time with the music. They picked up speed. Ryland never let go of both hands.

"This isn't so bad."

"You're doing great."

"Miss Jennalyn." Dawn caught up to them and turned to skate backward in front of them. "You're a natural."

"Says the girl who's been skating since she could walk." She raised Ryland's hand holding hers. "It's almost easy with a lifeline."

"She's right. You're good enough, strong enough, to do it on your own." Ryland squeezed her hand. "You don't need me."

But I want you. The self-admission stung with the pain of an internal thaw somewhere around her heart. She didn't *need* him. She proved that to herself every day that she didn't see him. She was beginning to wonder how much easier things would be with him. How much more enjoyable.

"It's not always about need." She smiled at Dawn and then Ryland. "You're right though. I should try to do this on my own."

Slowing their speed so they barely covered any distance, Jennalyn took a deep breath. She uncurled her fingers gripping Ryland's. He uncurled his. His palm still pressed against hers, offering support until she chose to let go.

When she did, Ryland and Dawn cheered her on with equal enthusiasm. They kept pace on either side of her as she sped up. Faster and faster until the air whipped at her hair and across her face. Her feet moved in a smooth glissade. A laugh, nothing more than a bubble of pleasure in her belly, swelled and rolled through her, pulling joy from the darkest corners of her soul until it erupted.

Dawn and Ryland laughed with her, and for the briefest moment when she looked at Dawn, she saw Sabrina with her glittering eyes, cherubic smile and infectious joy.

Instead of feeling sad, Jennalyn breathed in the moment and allowed herself to glide.

Chapter Eleven

The porch light shone its welcome when Ryland pulled into Jennalyn's drive. It was a sight he was growing to appreciate more and more. A sight he dreamed of on the days he didn't see her. Darkness dragged down those days, showed him the depth of naïveté he'd survived on.

He'd fallen in love before. Or so he'd thought. It became clear he'd been blinded by the idea of love. Looking from the porch to the woman in the seat beside him, temptation reared, paved the air. It was like the times he'd kissed her. And different.

She was the same caring woman with a generous spirit. Yet something had changed in her. The last two times they'd been together she'd opened up to him in ways that went beyond talking.

Instead, the insights she'd granted ran deeper. They offered glimpses into the pain she held hidden inside. Pain that centered around her parents almost as much as Sabrina. Sabrina's death still carried the most weight, if he read things right. Losing parents was a tragic loss, but it was a loss adults expected. Losing a younger sibling who was viewed as a child was much tougher. Especially considering that Sabrina had seemed okay after the accident.

Until discovering that she'd suffered an iceberg head injury.

Damage that couldn't be detected had hidden beneath the surface.

Love had given Jennalyn the strength to leave her job, risk her engagement and uproot her life for the sake of Sabrina and taking over the family business. The business was all she had left.

He rested his hand on her forearm, moved his fingers side to side. Satin skin with a tickling brush of fine hairs slipped against his palm and whispered suggestions along his mind.

"You're amazing."

"You've said that before." Her head lolled against the seat. Rather than look at him she watched his fingers move across her arm.

"I'm curious to see if there's a limit to how much you have to give."

"Yes."

He shook his head. "So you claim. But when you open yourself to others, you're still giving."

"What are you talking about?"

He slid his hand beneath hers so only their palms brushed. He didn't link their fingers or try to get closer. He only rested his palm beneath hers to feel her energy.

"Today, before you introduced Dawn to her idol, you allowed me to keep you from falling. You listened to Dawn's encouragement." Not that meeting Apolo Anton Ohno had been a hardship for Ryland. He loved watching the man skate.

"So? Introducing Dawn to Apolo was part of her miracle. As for letting you help me, that's taking, not giving."

"You gave us your trust." He leaned across the small distance that divided them and kissed her on the temple. Her hair smelled of vanilla and cinnamon as it brushed his nose. It reminded him of their food fight and the easy comfort of home during the holidays.

"I—"

"Opened yourself up to allow us into a sliver of your heart."

"Oh please." She might not have rolled her eyes, but the gesture was clear in her voice. "You must've hit your head on one of those falls."

"My head is fine." He pulled away long enough to get out and round the car to her side. She'd slid her coat back on by the time he opened the door. He helped her out before he continued with his point. "So is the rest of me."

"Then where's the medical-minded Ryland who analyzes the business side of healing?"

He placed his hands on the roof of the car, trapping her between him and the door. The desire to devour her ate at him, decimated his control. He lowered his head to her neck and nibbled at the patch of skin revealed by her scarf. "He doesn't exist around you."

"He didn't tell me he had a twin."

"I feel like I do." Leaning in, yet keeping a few inches between their bodies, he brushed the edge of her mouth with his lips. Energy rumbled to life inside him.

His blood sped. His pulse points thrummed harder.

"You make me want to play."

"I'm not playful."

"You have the capacity to be."

"How can you know that?"

"You soaked me during my magic show. You started a food fight. You went skating." He punctuated each statement with a touch or kiss. Each touch, kiss, had logic and desire colliding in his heart.

Logically, he didn't think she was ready for a relationship beyond what they had. Desire he couldn't avoid encouraged him to ignore logic.

She was a beautiful mystery that few men would understand. He did though.

"You have an infectious laugh." He tugged her scarf down, exposing the smooth skin of her throat. Captivated, he placed his mouth over the newly bared skin.

"You're mesmerizing."

He swept the tip of his tongue over her. She shivered. He shivered.

"You're like a drug that mellows me while filling me with giddiness." He angled his head, nuzzling at the bottom side of her jaw. "I suffer withdrawal when I leave you."

"It's been your choice each time you've left." Her hands rested on his shoulders. Her fingertips brushed his hair. "Well, except the time with the tree."

He shivered again.

"I won't take advantage of you while you're dealing with your grief."

"Grief is a part of my day, just as the sound of raw agony is a part of Riley." She dropped her head back, offered him a better advantage.

"You aren't always going to have such a tough month to cope with though."

"So you're waiting until I'm no longer stressed?" She pushed against him, nudging him back while a sudden drive to fight nagged. "Or do you see me as fragile?"

"I wouldn't say fragile." Word choice meant everything. The wrong response would have her turning away. It would lend a very literal meaning to being left in the cold.

What would you say? Her question was silent, but easily heard in her challenging stare.

"Grief makes us fragile in the way it isolates us, but that's more accurately a kind of loneliness."

"I'm not lonely, Ryland. Alone, yes. Lonely, no."

"That's a fine line of distinction." He took her hand, tucked it through his arm and then led her to the covered porch. "I want to be sure that if we move to a new level it's for the right reasons."

"And you think sex for the sake of sex or for the sake of sating a hunger is wrong."

"I prefer a little emotion."

On the porch, she turned and put her hand in his jacket pockets before stepping one pace closer. "I can promise emotion."

"But?" It was there. Twinkling as bright as the lights on neighboring homes. She had a condition.

"But while I am ready to explore this...attraction, I am not ready for forever."

"I'm not asking for forever." *Though more than just tonight would be nice.*

"Then it's agreed," she said as she casually unlocked and opened her front door.

"What?" He'd either missed something or she'd just agreed to sex. Images rushed into his mind in a flurry.

"We'll exchange emotions and see where it leads. Slowly."

She could be using him to fill a hole her family had once filled. She could be out for some relief and then she'd brush him off. She could be looking to scratch an itch left by her ex-fiancé.

Turning back, she hooked her fingers beneath his belt and
127

tugged him inside. He should argue, but his brain short-circuited like it had been interrupted by a defibrillator's jolt. He only registered that she was offering what he'd wanted since first meeting her. Why resist?

Decided, he leaned down and claimed her mouth in a kiss. He kicked the door closed behind him. A man could be noble for only so long.

Jennalyn gasped. Ryland's hands were gentle as he gripped her hips and pulled her against his body. His kiss was anything but the tender caress she'd grown to expect.

His urgency swept through her. She worked the buckle of his belt free and pulled the strip of leather from the loops in a yank that ended with a backlash slap against her thigh. The shocking sting of leather heightened her awareness.

Ryland shrugged out of his coat, dropped it on the floor and then removed hers. They hurried through the act of stripping one another of barriers. When they stood, short minutes later, naked, they paused for a deep breath and survey of bodies.

Peace eased through the room like a welcoming spirit. A first in over a year, Jennalyn was without the shadow of her past or of her family. She didn't carry the demands of running a business. Nothing mattered beyond the man before her and the way he made her feel.

And how he made her feel was...light. Free.

Knowing she couldn't explain herself, knowing there weren't enough of the right words in her purview, she took Ryland's hand in hers and led him to her room. With a not-so-gentle nudge, she pushed him onto the bed. He lay, gloriously naked and aroused, and waited for her with a smile on his kissable lips.

He wasn't thin or overly muscular, but his lean and nicely

toned body was evidence that he worked out and ate right. The understated power added to his appeal.

"You awaken a side of me I'd forgotten existed."

"I won't apologize for that."

"I'm not asking you to." She knelt between his legs and placed her hands on his knees. "Consider this a thank you."

"Jennalyn, I don't want—"

She leaned over and swiped her tongue along the length of him. His words died on a moan. She licked him again, swirling the tip of her tongue around the head of his erection. He arched his hips off the mattress. Her inner muscles clenched in anticipation. The thrill of arousing him was an arousal.

The flow of her body against his, skin to skin and heat to heat, beckoned. Answering passion's call, she took him in her mouth. Her jaw muscles protested the stretch required to accommodate his thickness. Even the minor discomfort was a pleasure, because it came with a feeling of pure goodness she'd been too long without.

Closing her eyes, hoping to lock the memory tight, she eased him out and in. He slid along the roof of her mouth, bumped the back of her throat. Shifting, she took him deeper until her gag reflex passed.

She'd always wondered what it would be like to cradle a man in her mouth, but she'd never felt comfortable enough to do it. Another barrier dropped away somewhere deep in her heart.

"Jennalyn." His hands fell to her shoulders. His fingers bit into her flesh. "You have to stop."

She sucked against him. Relished the jerk of him against her tongue. He flattened a palm on her head, stopping her ability to move.

"Are you trying to make me disgrace myself?" He sounded out of breath, like he'd been strangled, and his voice was raw.

She eased him out and wiggled up his body.

"An orgasm is never a disgrace." She punctuated each word with a kiss to his neck. He vibrated beneath her. His reactions fed hers and had her body responding in vibrations that struck deep in her tissues. Her inner walls clenched.

"I'm glad you feel that way." He flipped her to her back and jumped off the bed. After a quick trip to her closet, he returned with the belt to her robe.

"Ryland?"

"I have a fantasy that involves you, that iron headboard and a tie."

As if she couldn't tell from the gleam in his eyes, she asked, "What kind of fantasy?"

"The kind where you relinquish all control." He crawled onto the bed. She inched away from him, moving closer to the headboard. The idea excited and scared her simultaneously.

"Where you trust me fully with your safety and pleasure."

Worded like that, trust was the easiest thing to give him. He'd made her laugh, held her during her lowest moments and given her silent support when she'd battled emotions. He'd helped her rediscover the magic of what had promised to be a crappy time of year and shown her fun while promising more in his silvery eyes. Scooting back the last couple inches, she raised her hands over her head and gripped the rails.

"I'm all yours."

Grinning, he tied her up. He kept the tie loose, which meant she could change position if she wanted. Or he did it so she didn't feel too trapped. "How do you feel about a blindfold?"

"Go for it." The agreement—instant and excited—took her

off guard. She was agreeing to things she'd refused with past lovers.

After a quick kiss, he returned to her closet for a silk scarf. The moment he covered her eyes, her other senses kicked into high gear. She became aware of her body on a new level.

The smell of sex, or at least the scents she would now connect with sex, surrounded her. The cinnamon from her elf potpourri bowl mixed with the musk of Ryland's cologne. She breathed deep, drew the sensations and rich oxygen to her muscles. Her body relaxed as if she'd absorbed a heady drug.

The bed dipped and swayed as Ryland moved. Then there was no movement. His musky scent disappeared. The air stilled.

"Ryland?"

Silence.

He wouldn't have left her. Not after asking for her trust. But he wasn't answering.

"Ryland?"

Still he didn't answer. Her pulse kicked in a double beat. She was alone, blind and bound.

Then the air shifted again. It grew warmer. Friendlier.

She was no longer alone and the idea had her smiling. "You left me."

"Only for a minute." The edge of the bed dropped. "Did you miss me?"

"Strangely, yes." It wasn't actually so strange, but she wasn't going to think about that or share the admission and feed his ego.

He chuckled. It was a low rumble that shook her awareness and ramped up her curiosity.

"I wonder if you really missed me or if you thought I'd left

131

you."

She said nothing. She didn't need to because they both knew the truth. Her trust reached only so far. The day on the ice had made her look at who she trusted. She'd been able to think only of Chrissy. Until Ryland offered his hand. Knowing it now, she had no doubt where it had stemmed from. Kris. He had used Sabrina and the resulting demands on her time as a reason to have an affair. Opening herself up to more of the same did not sit high on Jennalyn's list.

"I am not going to abandon you..."

Ryland's whispered assurance trailed off as though he almost said more. He saw into her, but she wasn't the only one hesitant to share all of herself.

"I am going to make love to you though."

A rustle came from the bedside table. Plastic. And something else. Then a trail of ice-cold sensation swept across her breasts. She sucked in a breath, arched into the caress as her skin absorbed the moisture left behind by the ice.

Not seeing him or knowing what he'd do next was deliciously wicked. The scents grew richer. His touch hypnotized. She wanted more. She got more.

He trailed the ice around one nipple until it stood stiff and puckered. When he moved the ice around the second nipple his fingers replaced the ice on the first. They were as cold as the ice as he pinched her lightly.

She shook from head to toenail. Moving her hips, she tried to rub herself, to ease the ache throbbing between her legs. Only one thing would ease her desire, and she suspected he was going to make her wait a little longer.

"You're wet aren't you?"

She shifted again. Her slickened thighs rubbed easily

together. "Yes."

"You're going to be wetter before I take you."

She hadn't had a lot of lovers and none had talked during sex. It seemed naughty, and that thought only carried her deeper into his seductive web.

Delivering on unspoken promises that fulfilled those spoken, Ryland slid the shrinking ice between her breasts, down her stomach, over her pelvis and across her lower abdomen. A layer of cold lingered to be dried by the air. Her skin erupted with goose bumps. Each tiny bump became a supercharged nerve center. Then he pulled back.

Expecting him to move lower still, to use his icy fingers at the center of her ache, Jennalyn was stunned. He'd wanted her wetter. She was. So much so that she would certainly orgasm without him. If he'd read her that clearly and held himself on a tight enough leash to stop an onward plunge she was in real trouble.

Ryland was in real trouble.

He'd once thought the desire to kiss Jennalyn would pass after a kiss or two. That it had only made him want her with a gnawing hunger should have prepared him for the outcome of taking things further. A part of him had held on to the idea that he could keep things casual.

With her bound and blindfolded, waiting for his next touch, he accepted that things were not casual for him. He'd been tied up long before her. She could escape with a word. He would always be her captive.

"Ryland?"

Her questioning plea rescued him from his habit of overthinking things. *Doing* was a much more appealing thought.

"Turn over."

"Pardon?"

It was excitement not fear that he heard in her voice. The same excitement roared in his veins, bubbling and heating his body, filling his brain. He had to expel a pent-up breath before he could speak.

"Turn over." He phrased the request like a gentle command. He would accept her refusal if she put it out there, but he hoped she didn't.

"I'm tied up."

"You're loose enough. The belt will twist and allow you to hold the bar."

"As you wish." The corner of her lip twitched. She liked whatever images filled her head. "You want me flat or on my knees?"

His arousal—already a bit painful from his restraint—thickened. "Do you have a preference?"

"I couldn't say."

"You've never..." He closed his eyes, bit his lip. The woman was giving him all the power. Maybe he'd be less inclined to take her like an animal the moment she turned over if her gloriously curved ass wasn't sticking in the air. "Flat."

"As you wish." She turned over and wiggled into the pillows to settle comfortably.

Her naked backside and a spear-shaped birthmark riding high on one butt cheek taunted him. Fisting his hands for a moment, he prayed for control he wasn't sure would last if it came. With a bump of his knee against the inside of hers, she spread her legs. Ryland nestled himself between her warm thighs. The arousal glistening on her silken skin captivated him.

An idea came to Ryland, daring him to make all kinds of crazy demands to see where her limits were. How much could he ask for before she stopped quoting *The Princess Bride*?

He released a long exhale as he bent over and placed his hands on either side of her for support. The urge to devour ravaged his body, attacking his restraint faster than a parasite eating through antibodies.

He was helpless against the inevitable. He didn't want a cure.

Intent on kissing her neck, he lowered himself. His mouth pressed against her skin. The kiss became a nibble. The nibble became a need to suck until he marked her.

She arched into him, plastering her body to his. Back to chest, ass to dick, thigh to thigh. Snug against her with his blood becoming an inferno of hormones, Ryland was sure he'd burn. He sucked harder. She writhed, trying to get closer.

His lungs seized. On a gasp he pushed off her. The move only pressed his lower body more firmly against hers. Clenched teeth were no match for his need, but damn if his jaw didn't shake beneath the force.

Shoving back to sit on his heels, he broke all contact. The move might have given him enough distance to breathe a few deep breaths. All it really did was give him a clear view of Jennalyn's swollen sex. Waiting. Calling.

He grabbed the condom he'd dropped on the bed earlier and ripped it open. The thin layer of rubber promised no help in lasting longer, because even the brush of his own fingers as he rolled the protection into place had the pressure building.

"Ryland." Jennalyn shifted, raising her hips off the bed.

"Yes?" The word became strangled as it shoved through his closing windpipe.

"Hurry up."

"Bossy." Easing forward, he lifted her into his lap. Her thin legs stretched along either side of his hips.

"You're taking too long." Her body echoed her claim as she shifted higher, rubbing her weeping center against him.

He squeezed his eyes closed. His jaw shook harder.

She shifted again.

His back muscles spasmed. Low. Hot.

With a growl, he grabbed her hips and drove into her. One thrust to the hilt wasn't enough. Two, three and four weren't enough. He could spend hours inside her and still crave her.

She matched his pace, moving with him in perfect sync. Each glide against her squeezing walls pushed him a little closer to the ledge. Sweat dampened his hairline. Ran down his neck.

Jennalyn grabbed a rail of the headboard and pulled herself up. The shift buried him deeper. His balls tightened with the coming orgasm. Fire raged in and around him. He took her breasts in his hands, savoring the way their bodies fit while trying to be gentle, but the passionate moan that escaped her shattered his intentions. Massaging, squeezing tighter, he thrust deeper.

The world erupted into shards of vibrant color as he followed her around the orgasmic bend.

Chapter Twelve

The leafless trees lining the sidewalks of the Circle were wrapped in multi-hued Christmas lights. Festive lights and wreaths, trees and holiday-themed windows surrounded them while cheerful carols crescendoed and faded as shop doors opened and closed. Across the Circle, the windows of an office building had been covered with a large white screen that would show *It's A Wonderful Life* as soon as it was dark enough.

People were scouting seats on the steps of the Circle, covering them with pillows, quilts and padded seats for comfort. The efforts for comfort and the layers of clothes needed for warmth would lose importance when the Circle swelled with the crowds of people. The spirit of the festivities would fill the air as intangible but as real as oxygen.

Enjoying the relaxed mood and some window-shopping, Ryland and Jennalyn walked along the outer sidewalks. Viv, a girl who was seeing her first Christmas clearly thanks to a cornea transplant, walked between them. Viv's parents had scouted out the perfect spot for the movie where they could lean against the base of the monument. They held the seats while Jennalyn and Ryland took Viv to see the theatrics that was the Circle at Christmas.

It was almost as grand as Main Street at Disney during the night parade. Shop owners set up booths outside their stores, giving away cups of hot chocolate, apple cider and eggnog. A small bar even gave away hot toddies to interested adults. A candy store gave away Christmas-themed candies and The Chocolate Cafe gave out sample after sample.

"I look at this every day, but I've never seen it as I see it tonight." Ryland said quietly.

"Ryland." A man who looked to be in his late forties smiles as he passed a bag of Christmas pretzels to Viv. "You find you some women to share the movie with you?"

"Luckily." Ryland made brief introductions to the café's manager and then steered them on.

"Joshua seems nice."

"He is. But he'd keep us talking all through the movie if we let him." The statement was made with fondness, so Jennalyn knew Ryland liked the man.

Viv pulled the attention back to her and talked about anything and everything that came to mind. As seemed to be the case with most seven-year-olds, a lot of things popped into her mind. The night's fun came from seeing everything as Viv saw them. Before she could remember seeing the sights of Christmas, her corneas had begun to deteriorate. Without a vision-saving transplant she'd have gone blind, but she'd received her Christmas miracle.

"I can't decide if I like the white lights or the colored lights the best," Viv prattled on as she wound a piece of cinnamon cotton candy around her tiny finger. "The white ones I like in the fake snow. They make everything sparkly."

"But the colored ones?" Ryland's question was for Viv, but the smile in his eyes was for Jennalyn as they both recalled a similar conversation.

"The colored ones are so fun. When they do their blink blink blink it makes me think of fairies dancing. Like maybe
138

they've been trapped inside the little glass cover and want to get free."

"My sister loved the colored ones the best. Only her opinion was that each light was a wish an angel had granted." Jennalyn allowed Sabrina's theory to push Viv's sadder one aside. Hoping to pull Viv to her way of thinking, she stopped by a pole wrapped in a strand of fat colored lights. "Maybe one of these is shining in celebration of your eyes."

Viv studied the bulbs for a moment. Her head cocked a little to the right and she stuck her lower lip out a tad. Jennalyn could all but hear the hum of her thoughts as she considered the new possibility. It didn't matter if she chose to adopt Sabrina's theory or not, it was still Jennalyn's preference.

"Trapped fairies do seem a little sad now that I think about it." Viv nodded, first slowly and then more enthusiastically. "Yeah. I like the granted wishes better."

"It's a beautiful sentiment." Ryland slid a hand beneath Jennalyn's scarf and gave her neck a light squeeze. "I would even go so far as to suggest that the clear ones are tears of the same angels because while they can't grant every wish, every wish deserves to be recognized."

Viv shrugged and walked on a couple steps ahead of them. Dancing reindeer in a window captured her attention and had her telling a story about a Christmas concert at school the year before. The kids wore their pajamas and reindeer antlers while they sang "Rudolph the Red-Nosed Reindeer". Her delight at the memory was infectious, but Ryland's explanation of the lights resonated.

Sabrina and their mother had come up with the explanation of the colored lights. It had always made Jennalyn smile to hear them make up stories about possible wishes. She'd never given any thought to the same kind of game in regards to the clear lights. Now that Ryland had planted the seed, though, it had taken root.

Every flicker of white resembled a glistening tear someone had shed. It was sad, but the colored lights offered the uplifting side. For every tear there was something to smile about. Something to celebrate.

Jennalyn slipped her hand into her pocket and rubbed her gloved thumb over the crackled quartz Ryland had given her the night before. He'd explained that the green stone helped open the heart chakra. With the heart chakra open and healthy it was easier to accept love and friendship. Rubbing the stone now, though she couldn't actually feel the glide of the polished surface against the pad of her thumb, she embraced the calming sensation that swept over her.

"You've gone quiet." Ryland spoke low and close to her ear. The smile that hadn't left his face or his voice had grown subdued.

"Just thinking."

"Remembering?"

She nodded toward Viv. "Sabrina chattered from one topic to another like that. Few things would hold her focus for more than a few minutes before she'd jump to the next story."

"It was part of her charm. Just as it's part of Viv's."

Ryland's hand still rested warm and sure on her neck. His touch roused her awareness on one level while helping her relax on another. He'd proved himself to be a generous lover, but more importantly he was showing himself to be a great friend.

He seemed to understand her and her hesitations. He didn't push when she wanted to pull back, but he didn't allow her to retreat when she needed to move forward. It was a balancing act she'd witnessed while watching her parents. It was something she'd always wanted, but had never actually

140

found.

The taste of it now was a tempting draw she wasn't sure she would be able to walk away from when A Month of Miracles ended.

"Oh my gosh!" Viv's exclamation pitched on a high squeal on the last syllable. She stopped before a window filled with glass statues. She flattened her hands on the glass and pressed her nose to the pane. "Look at them."

Frolicking in and over a thick bed of artificial snow was a family of fairies. Like the lights all around, the fairies were an array of colors that ranged from pale to vibrant. There were boy and girl fairies. They ran and skipped and jumped rope. Others, the ones suspended from thin wire, soared or dove or danced in the air.

"Their wings are so pretty."

"Do you have a favorite?" Ryland asked.

"That one." Viv pointed at a blue fairy so light it was almost clear. Spread wide to the sides and opened at the tips in wide fans that led to five detailed points, each wing curved in what looked like an invitation for a hug. "Look at her eyes."

Following Viv's instruction, Jennalyn looked at the eyes. They were a brilliant blue, almost teal, with a few flecks of silver shooting through the irises. "She's stunning. The artist didn't miss a detail."

"Not one," Ryland agreed with Jennalyn as he moved toward the shop door. "I think this fairy needs a home." He winked at Viv as she followed him. "Maybe with a young girl who will always admire her?"

"Do you mean it?" Viv's voice whisked across the air, shocked and hopeful.

"Of course I do. I also think she should have a friend or

two." Ryland brushed a gloved hand over the girl's hair, hesitating just long enough for Jennalyn to wonder if he was imagining how things might have been with Elise. When he pulled his hand away, rubbing the tips of his fingers together as if he was savoring a moment he already missed, she had no doubt.

The man's generosity was boundless, but it was nothing compared to how he would have been if his own daughter had lived. Elise Davids would have been a seriously cherished fairy princess.

The movie played across the screen-covered building with Jimmy Stewart's voice coming through the speakers that had been placed throughout the Circle. Ryland and Jennalyn sat to the left of Viv and her parents.

The press of Jennalyn's body against Ryland as his arm circled her and held her close to his side negated the discomfort of sitting on concrete steps. Her warmth penetrated the layers of clothes and eased into him. Angling his head, he rubbed his cheek along the top of Jennalyn's. The softness of her knitted hat tickled. It was a simple pleasure he hadn't expected to find during A Month of Miracles.

He enjoyed every moment with her. Whether they were in a crowded arena, a firehouse having a food fight, decorating the Christmas tree in her living room or sitting on cold concrete with thousands of other people, he enjoyed her. Through no intention of her own, she helped him embrace fun. The days grew brighter, and each one with her near had him wanting more desperately to make sure Jennalyn enjoyed as many moments as possible.

Rubbing his cheek against her again, he breathed her in.

Her scent wafted around him. Her spirit—sexy compassion— whispered through him.

"You're a nice guy, Ryland Davids."

Ryland flexed the arm he had around her shoulders, brought her closer for a beat. "You're not so bad yourself, Jennalyn James."

They spoke in undertones, trying not to disturb the other movie watchers. "You would have spoiled Elise rotten."

Talking about his daughter and how things might have been should hurt. He never talked about her because of the expectation of pain. With Jennalyn there was only a feeling of rightness. "What makes you think that?"

"Viv only had to say the fairies were pretty and you were taking her inside to buy her some."

"She wanted one, even if she was too polite to ask."

"But you didn't stop at one." Jennalyn lifted a hand and covered his.

Her fingers curled into the curve of his palm, linking them for however long she was willing. She had allowed him into her bed and to spend the night. She'd been genuine, but a part of her had pulled back the moment he released the tie.

"I like to see beautiful girls smile."

"You seem to have a knack for making it happen."

"You sound as if that's a bad thing."

"Not bad." She shrugged, her shoulder rising and falling against his. "Just another layer of your perfection."

He chuckled. "I am not perfect."

"Says the man paying for A Month of Miracles out of his pocket when he could use hospital funds."

"Shh. We agreed to keep that between us."

"I've told no one."

"Not even Chrissy?"

"Not even Chrissy." Shaking her head, she sighed. "Though I don't fully understand the secrecy. And the accounting department at the hospital surely knows."

"These gifts are typically easier for people to accept when they seem less..."

"Involved?"

"Personal."

"No." She shook her head, stopping with her face half buried in his neck. "I don't buy that reason."

"Are you calling me a liar?"

"I've spent enough time with people to come to a different conclusion."

"Like what?"

"You don't want them to know *you* are the one granting their miracles."

"If that was so true I wouldn't be so openly generous with the gifts."

"Please. You know as well as I do that they think you're spending hospital money. That's when they think about the financial side of things."

"You think too much." And her thoughts hit too closely to home. People in his position were expected to make a lot of money. The reality of it either attracted people who thought negatively about the wealthy or those who wanted special favors.

"I think you're too perfect."

"I swear I'm not."

She shook her head again and shifted her gaze back to the

movie. For the rest of the movie and then through the process of getting out of the crowds, Jennalyn spoke only to Viv and her parents. When they'd split off from the Nortons, Jennalyn slid back into silence.

She still hadn't said anything more when Ryland pulled into her driveway and slipped the car into park. The silence, which hadn't bothered him before, began to wiggle beneath his skin in a discomforting way.

Staring forward, he drummed his fingers on the wheel. He wanted to say something that would make sure the night didn't have to end. Simultaneously, he couldn't presume he had an automatic invitation to follow her inside. He needed her to know she had her space even if he preferred she not take advantage of it.

God, he hated complications.

Nothing was coming to him, so he resorted to what made sense and came easily. He reached into his pocket, pulled out the gemstone he'd picked out for her and offered her the iridescent rock.

"Ryland?"

"It's a tiger's eye." Thinking about the meaning was a reminder that he needed to be like the animal the stone was named for. Patient.

"And you picked it out because..."

"Tigers are known for their strong determination and patience. They can focus on a desire for days at a time until they attain even the most impossible."

She looked from the stone still in his palm to him. "You have to have a flaw."

"Didn't we go through this earlier?"

"And yet you continue to show how great you are."

"For the record," he whispered as he placed the stone in her hand. "You're pretty fabulous yourself."

Jennalyn said nothing. Instead, she drew in a deep breath and held it for a few beats before slowly exhaling. "Speaking of desire, there's something I've been thinking of."

"Really?" He traced the edge of her ear and lingered, rubbing the patch of skin showing above her scarf. "You going to tell me about it?"

"Maybe." She covered his hand with hers and leaned across the dividing distance. Squeezing his fingers, she eased closer to the console. Closer to him.

He shifted closer until he bumped the console. He rested his left hand on her hip. The warmth that was becoming a commonality when around Jennalyn sparked into flames of desire. Orbs of light floated across his field of vision, illuminating her in a halo of brilliance.

"Do you want to come inside?"

He didn't miss the implication of her question, or the fact that she was still holding something back. Neither would he leave her and miss a moment of the pleasure he found in her company. "I would love to come inside."

Chapter Thirteen

Mass Ave Toys had been transformed from its typical toyland to a winter toyland. Stepping through the glass doors was like stepping onto a movie set for the toyshop at the North Pole.

Toys of every size, shape and type were everywhere. Children-centric Christmas carols, currently one by the Chipmunks, played through the sound system. The staff was dressed like pointy-eared elves wearing red aprons covered with embroidered candy canes spelling their names.

White twinkle lights wrapped the red support beams, turning them into floor-to-ceiling candy canes. Stuffed animals and baby dolls wore miniature Santa hats or held the reins to reindeer. The windows had been painted for the holiday.

The paintings along the front of the building brought the toys inside to life as they engaged in a snowball fight with different parts of Mass Ave behind them. The large arched window inside had been decorated with a Norman Rockwell–type scene where a man handed a stuffed bear to a child in a wheelchair.

"This place looks amazing." Jennalyn scanned the store, taking in every detail her brain could process.

"Thank you. I'm glad you like it." Angela, the store's manager, greeted her with a smile and firm handshake.

"Love, not like. Angela, it's Christmas perfection."

"We have the sleigh all set up for Nancy's signing."

Jennalyn followed Angela around the fun and playful toy displays to the open space in the middle of the store where a life-sized sleigh dominated, but instead of reindeer two miniature ponies were hitched to it. Itty, a palomino the color of hay with a white mane and tail was on the right. Bitty, a black pony with a white sock on his back right foot was on the left. Each one had white spots on their coat, just as they did in the books about their adventures.

The unique part about the sleigh was that the doublewide bench seat had a shelf type desk that extended from the back for half the seat. It was the perfect setup for an author appearance, because the author could sit on the inside and sign the book while the visiting child could sit beside them. Pictures turned out perfectly, without the worry of trying to find a convenient way for kids to stand beside the author.

"Chrissy told me you were doing amazing things in here." Jennalyn ran a hand along the mane of Itty. "This is beyond amazing."

Mass Ave Toys's owner had proven herself to be a brilliant business owner over the last several years. Jennalyn had chosen her store because of its stellar reputation and the confidence that the staff would put a great event together. The transformation they'd put the store through surpassed the highest expectation.

"I couldn't have done it without an awesome staff. The funding from A Month of Miracles certainly didn't hurt."

"Ryland is all about granting dreams this month."

"Speaking of that." Angela set to work tweaking the display of Itty and Bitty books around the sleigh. "In addition to the first hundred kids receiving a free book, every parent who brings a child in today, even after the signing, will receive fifty dollars in merchandise."

"That's new."

Angela smiled. "A Month of Miracles has taken on a life of its own."

"Chrissy mentioned that it was getting a bit of publicity."

"A bit?" Angela asked. "Jennalyn, you can't turn on the TV or radio or pick up a paper without seeing or hearing about it."

"I've been so wrapped up in the individual events, I guess I've been in a bit of a bubble."

"Welcome to the reality of what you've helped kick off. Clubs, associations and businesses all around the area are doing things on their own to grant wishes."

Chrissy had tried to tell Jennalyn about the publicity, but she had been distracted by the events, the kids she'd been meeting and Ryland. When she made it into the office she was swept into a haze of calls from new clients and working on the finishing touches of A Month of Miracles. Leaving the details of the business to Chrissy for the month, she'd apparently missed the magnitude of how much momentum A Month of Miracles was picking up.

"And this is your gift?"

"Mine and about twenty other businesses who went in with me."

"Wow." It had occurred to her to ask for sponsorships. She'd suggested it in the early planning stages, but Ryland had requested that they keep things a little lower key. It seemed the low-key approach wasn't working out as he'd hoped.

"Given the circumstances, I was a little surprised when Ryland asked that I not mention his name in the press release for today."

"He didn't want the publicity?"

"Apparently not, but I'm not sure he's going to be able to avoid it. There are some big-name sponsors backing us."

"I'm sure he'll handle it."

Thirty minutes later when Ryland walked into the toy store, Jennalyn was still surprised by what she'd learned. Approaching him while Angela worked to get the guest author, Nancy Carpenter Czera set up, Jennalyn debated whether or not to ask about the media.

"You've knocked another one out of the park, Jennalyn."

"I only picked the location and the author. The rest was Angela and the staff."

"Modesty. I like it."

As simple as that, the decision was made for her. "Speaking of modesty, why haven't you mentioned how much attention this month has been getting?"

The too-perfect man who'd been whittling his way beneath her skin shrugged. The shrug was his pink-cheeked show of embarrassment. "We talked about this."

She glanced around to make sure they were secluded enough not to be overheard by the mingling shoppers. "We talked about you not wanting people to know you were footing the bill. We didn't talk about why you want to keep it a secret that *you* thought up A Month of Miracles."

"Jennalyn."

"Someone is going to out you, Ryland. Possibly today."

"No."

"Do you know that Angela has twenty additional sponsors for today? They're giving every parent who walks in this door a certificate for fifty dollars so that every child has a special gift under their tree this year. The media isn't going to skip covering a day like today."

"The patients I've invited will not give anyone my name. I expect the same from you." His tone hardened, allowing no room for argument.

Then, before she could respond, he turned and walked away, heading toward two kids who'd just come into the store with their families. He smiled at the girl who couldn't be more than five and the boy who was maybe three. Something was off about the way Ryland moved, but Jennalyn couldn't see past the distraction of agony that ripped through her heart as if she'd been stabbed by a heated ice pick.

She was okay with his stance on his privacy.

She was not okay with the unspoken suggestion that she would be the one to reveal his identity.

He'd made a point of asking for her trust, of letting her know she was safe with him, but when the moment came to test her he doubted his decision to give her the same. How could he ask her to give him something he wouldn't give in return? And why should she consider giving it?

Tension pinched the muscles between Ryland's shoulder blades and radiated up his neck. The day had started out on a low with news that Bria, the little girl who'd been so joyous during the magic show a few short weeks ago, had suffered a setback in her health. Things weren't looking good for her, and though the news was to be expected given his job, the expectation never made the sadness easier to take.

Topping off the unnecessary pain of a child he'd come to care personally for with the idea that he might be announced as the backer to A Month of Miracles toppled things into the shitty category. He couldn't think about the possibility of being revealed or the ramifications of what might happen if he was.

His focus needed to be on the reasons he was at Mass Ave Toys. Blake and Paige were receiving their miracles.

Blake, a three-year-old who'd received bone grafts to correct tumors that weakened his legs, was walking on his own. He was pain-free and ready to tackle the world without the need of constant worry that his bones would break. His miracle was getting to shop for whatever toys he could want that didn't require him to be sitting still.

At five, Paige had suffered acute liver failure after being given the wrong dosage of acetaminophen. The girl loved horses, wanted a pony desperately, but was very allergic. Meeting the author of the Itty and Bitty stories and getting to go home with the stuffed versions of the miniatures was her miracle.

They were a couple of his favorite success stories. Today more than most, he needed the reminder that not all the cases in his hospital ended in death.

He knelt between the two of them and asked, "Are you two ready for a great time?"

"Yes, sir."

"Super." He turned to Blake and smiled. "Blake, you get to go shopping with your parents. Play with the toys here until you can't stand it any longer. Then I want to hear all about your favorites. This will help Santa know what to bring you."

"'Kay." The little boy left with his parents, who led the way to the outdoor toys.

Ryland lifted Paige into his arms and headed toward the pony-drawn sleigh. "There's someone here today I think you'll enjoy meeting."

"Who?"

Rounding the corner of a display, he pointed to the sleigh.

Paige looked at the author sitting in the bench with a book in her lap, at the ponies, then back at the author and then back at the ponies again. A grin stretched across her face.

"That's Itty and Bitty," she whispered.

"It is. The woman in the sleigh writes their stories. She knows the real Itty and Bitty."

Paige wiggled free and slid to the floor before he could say more. With no hesitation or fear of the unknown, she hurried into the sleigh with Nancy. Leaving the supervision of Paige to her parents, Ryland eased away and went to watch Blake play.

He was leaning against the wall, watching the two kids, making mental notes of the things that seemed to excite them most, when the air shifted, warmed.

Jennalyn.

"I think I found your flaw," she said as she leaned against the wall beside him.

"What's that?"

"You become the proverbial bear when backed into a corner."

He resisted a snort. Barely. "How so?"

"One hint that your generosity may be found out by the masses and your hackles rise."

"Sounds more like a porcupine."

"That image works too." She slid a step closer. "Wanna tell me what is really bothering you?"

"No." Talking about his mood meant thinking about Bria. Thinking about Bria meant thinking about what was happening with her. That would have his focus shifting back to the hospital and images of her too weak to do anything for herself.

"Is it really the idea of people finding out about you?"

"No." That was an easy truth. "Now please let it drop so I can enjoy the day."

"Fine." She pointed toward Paige in the sleigh with Nancy. "Did you know Nancy wrote a special story for Paige? Itty and Bitty take her on one of their adventures."

"That was sweet of her." It would have taken a lot of time and effort, and the layer of devotion to a young girl the author had never met pleased him. Even the extra touching gift didn't brighten the dullness of the day, though.

"You know what else is sweet?"

"What?"

"You, despite your bad mood."

"Drop it, Jennalyn."

"Hmm, no." She turned to face him, leaning against the wall on a shoulder instead of her back. "You have to know how far the inspiration of A Month of Miracles is reaching."

He shrugged.

"Why didn't you tell me?"

"Our goal is the same. To provide a perfect day for a few special kids."

"Are you worried that people will come ask you for money if they know what you're doing?"

"A little." The tension in his back tightened. He really wanted her to drop the subject. "Listen, I need to get to the hospital. Can you handle...?" He waved at Blake and Paige, trusting Jennalyn to know what he wanted.

"Sure."

"Thanks." He reached into his pocket, pulled out a small box and handed it to her. Without another word, he walked away.

Jennalyn watched Ryland until he'd left the store and was out of view of the window before she opened the hinged lid of the box. A note, written in Ryland's bold, almost unreadable handwriting was tucked into the lid.

I already gave you an amethyst, I know. But it suited you so well, I wanted you to have something as special as you. A one of a kind.

Ryland

Jennalyn pulled a ring from the box and slid it on. Thin wire wrapped her finger in several loops making one. It then moved up to circle the crackled, purple stone in several rough twists before crossing across the top to hold the stone in place. Its roughness was its beauty.

A sense of emotional comfort settled deeper than she'd have thought possible.

Ryland granted a different wish every time she saw him. Wishes she didn't realize she had. The least she could do was make sure Paige and Blake enjoyed the perfect day while protecting Ryland's privacy.

After she did that, she would find a way to make his day better.

Chapter Fourteen

Jennalyn had wondered what the perfect gift for Ryland might be, because the more she thought about it the more she came to realize that in all the time they'd spent together he revealed very little about himself.

She'd called his office to be told he was somewhere in the hospital, but his secretary didn't know where. She'd called his cell phone several times to be routed immediately to his voicemail. She'd have gone to his house, but didn't know where he lived.

The man's quest for privacy wasn't isolated to how he spent his money.

Defeated, Jennalyn approached her front porch. Ryland saw into the heart of what motivated her so clearly, but she couldn't read him. He was sweet, funny and generous, but that didn't help her figure out where he would go for peace when he was having a crap day.

Her thoughts were derailed when she reached the house. Taped above the handle of the door was a DVD. She closed her eyes and traced a fingertip around the edge of the disc. The man needed someone to be there for him, to listen as he talked about whatever had been bothering him, but he instead made sure to give *her* a gift. And he'd made sure to get what had to be a message from Sabrina onto her door.

Opening her eyes, Jennalyn pulled the disc free and headed inside. She didn't take the time to change into her robe or get a glass of wine. She didn't even kick off the heels she'd worn all day. She was more curious about what Sabrina would say this time. How would it tie into how things were going, because so far her sister had shown an eerie insight?

Hitting play on the remote as soon as the TV and DVD player were ready, Jennalyn lowered herself to the edge of the couch. Sabrina's face, pale and a little confused, came into view.

"Whenever you're ready, Sabrina." Ryland's voice, calm and encouraging, slid into the living room, into Jennalyn, as if he were sitting beside her. He spoke more carefully than other times. He was being gentle because Sabrina was getting worse.

Jennalyn had discovered a flaw in him, but it only made him more endearing when she weighed it against his spirit.

"JJ," Sabrina began. "It's getting harder for me to remember stuff, but you know that."

Her lips barely moved to form the words that slurred into each other. The video had been made in Sabrina's last days. The messy speech had been one of the final signs of her brain deterioration, but the knowledge didn't carry the same sadness this time.

"I don't know how much longer I have, so this is going to be my last DVD. Besides, Ryland says he's tired of me making him cry."

"Hey!" Ryland chastised Sabrina from off screen. "You promised."

"Sorry. I promise not to tell her that you disappear to the roof of your apartment building when you leave me."

"Do a man's secrets mean nothing to you?"

"Is it going to matter if I tell her these things? She's going to be dealing with her own issues when you give this to her." Sabrina shrugged. "Besides, it's not like I have your address to give her."

"There is that."

"I know only that you overlook the war memorial and seem to see James Whitcomb Riley everywhere you go."

"You're a brat, Sabrina."

She laughed at his playfulness. "You still love me."

"Impossible not to. Do you have a message for your sister? Or is your parting gift a lesson in giving me a hard time?"

"It's a good gift if she's going to spend any time with you." Sabrina shifted her gaze to look more directly at Jennalyn. "He likes when I pick on him, JJ."

"He picks back, Sab." Jennalyn laughed.

Her baby sister had suffered more moments of forgetfulness the closer she'd gotten to the end, but when she was lucid she was very lucid. And she'd never lost her self or her spunk. Her passion for life.

"He mostly likes to make me laugh, which is what I want for you." Sabrina grew serious. "Don't forget to laugh, even when it feels like you're losing the silent battle inside."

Jennalyn turned off the DVD player and stared at the TV thinking about Sabrina's message. It wasn't anything she hadn't said in person, but the reminder was a good one. There had been many days Jennalyn had become too overwhelmed by the war within to remember to laugh. Ryland had been in the same frame of mind earlier.

I look at this every day, but I've never seen it this way. His words from the movie in the Circle came back to her and mixed with Sabrina's teasing.

Ryland lived on the Circle. He had to if he was close enough to see the lights every day. And he knew the man at The Chocolate Café. He likely had a view of the James Whitcomb Riley statue. He likely lived very close to the Circle.

Determined to find him, to make sure he took the advice he helped Sabrina pass on, Jennalyn grabbed her keys and headed downtown for the second time that day. By the time she made it through traffic and found a parking spot, darkness had set in. With the setting of the sun, the temperatures had dropped.

They only promised to drop more with the expected ten to twelve inches of snow that were supposed to fall overnight. The coming snow wasn't too unusual in the area, but it still had the streets fuller than normal as people tried to make sure they had everything they could need. She cared only about getting to Ryland.

Another call sent straight to voicemail ramped up her frustration and her determination to find him. Two things she'd picked up about Ryland were that he had a sweet tooth and he liked coffee. Specifically, he liked coffee from The Chocolate Café enough so that the manager knew him by name.

Ready to bribe the manager with a large sale if necessary, Jennalyn headed to The Chocolate Café. Talking about walking the Circle and watching the movie with Ryland, she made sure the manager remembered her from a few nights before.

"Jennalyn." Joshua, the manager who clearly had a crush on Ryland despite the fact they played for different teams, grew more open with every kind of chocolate Jennalyn purchased. "You're helping Ryland with A Month of Miracles."

"It's sort of become a pet project."

"He's told me about the great things you've come up with for the kids." Joshua tied a colorful bow around a bag of Christmas pretzels. "My partner's favorite was the concert with

Idina Menzel. Though, personally, meeting Apolo Anton Ohno would have been awesome."

"They were both pretty great."

The chimes over the door jingled, announcing another customer. Joshua greeted them, saying he'd be right with them. Jennalyn moved to the register as Joshua began ringing up her purchases. She was about to try talking him out of Ryland's address when he leaned across the counter with a hopeful look.

"Are you by any chance going upstairs to see Ryland?"

"It was my plan, but I don't know his apartment number."

"If I gave it to you would you be willing to deliver his coffee? I had some staff call in sick and can't get it to him. I was hoping he would come in for it like he normally does, but he hasn't."

"Of course." Less than five minutes later she reached for Ryland's doorbell with the hope that he wouldn't be mad that she'd tracked him down.

Her wait was brief, barely long enough to lower her hand and shift the box of chocolate and coffee that she carried. The door swung open and a stunning blonde woman, maybe five years younger than Ryland, greeted her with a confused yet pleasant look.

"Can I help you?" The woman asked.

"I have a delivery for Ryland Davids."

The blonde held a hand out. "I'll see that he gets it."

"Um, if it's okay I would like to give it to him personally." *I want to look him in the eye when I ask who you are.*

Jennalyn hated thinking that Ryland's big flaw was the same flaw Kris had had. The woman blocking his doorway with suspicion growing in her gaze had Jennalyn's inner alarms blaring. The last man she'd trusted had betrayed her by cheating. Ryland had worked at getting her to open up, to trust him, and now a woman was answering his door.

It didn't look good.

"He's really not in the mood for company tonight."

The stubbornness she'd inherited from her mother was rearing up. Jennalyn wouldn't walk away from Ryland's door until she knew the identity of this other woman. Or until she knew if she was the other woman. "I'll make it quick."

"Just a minute." The blonde closed the door, leaving Jennalyn in the hall.

A long minute later the door opened again. Ryland stood before her with bloodshot and swollen eyes. He said nothing, only swallowed and opened the door wider, stepping back for her to pass.

Jennalyn's heart shuddered at the raw pain surrounding him. He closed the door behind her and silently led the way into the stark living room that showed no personality aside from the Christmas tree that sat dark. It wasn't what she'd have expected from the man who dressed up like a clown to entertain kids or who spent so much energy making her feel special. Instead, his home filled her with loneliness. Made her wonder if he was the lonelier of the two of them.

"Ryland?"

He pointed at the blonde woman who'd dropped into a white armchair. "This is Michele. My sister. Michele, Jennalyn."

His sister. Now that he said it Jennalyn could see the resemblance between them, and she felt ridiculous for having distrusted him. For having been jealous.

Michele nodded politely, but she didn't get up to shake Jennalyn's hand. Neither of them wasted breath on the standard it's-nice-to-meet-you greeting. Whatever was going on, there was nothing nice about the mood in Ryland's apartment.

Jennalyn set the box she carried on a nearby table and turned to Ryland. Instinct had her reaching for his hand to offer him comfort as he had her. "What's happened?"

"A patient passed away this evening."

"Oh, no." Tears flooded her eyes as instantly as the memory of agonizing wails and crushing pain moved in. She went to him, wrapped her arms around his waist. "I'm so sorry."

"It was Bria. The little girl from..."

"...the magic show." The little girl whose laugh had delighted Jennalyn as they soaked Ryland. "What can I do?"

As she asked the question she knew it was ridiculous. There was nothing she could do to ease his sadness. He'd told her how rarely he allowed himself to get close to patients, but Bria had obviously wound her way into his heart, just as Sabrina had. He felt the pain of loss as completely as he would have felt Elise's or Sabrina's.

"Have you eaten?"

He said nothing, so Michele answered. "He won't let me order him anything."

Jennalyn fought back the tears, pulling herself under control for both their sakes, and led him to the couch. He sank like he was weighted down.

"You're going to eat."

"There's food here. I'll eat when I'm hungry." He moved his gaze from Jennalyn to his sister to Jennalyn. "I've seen you in a kitchen, and she can't boil water."

Jennalyn remembered the hours, hell, the days, after Sabrina died. She would have starved if it hadn't been for neighbors and Chrissy bringing her food. Ryland was functioning better than she had, but the loss was still hitting him hard.

"I'm not completely worthless. Point me to the kitchen."

Michele stood. "I'll show you around."

Jennalyn grabbed the box she'd brought in with her. Before going with Michele, she pulled out the chocolate toy soldier she'd bought. Handing it to Ryland, she kissed him on the temple and whispered in his ear, "You're my hero."

The white, contemporary kitchen was large with top-notch appliances, but the utilitarian impression that had greeted her in the living room didn't persist here. Pots and pans with scars and dings hung from a rack over the stove. An industrial mixer with a large stainless steel bowl sat on the counter. Beside it sat Michele's picture. Tucked into the corner of Michele's picture was a small print of Sabrina.

"Oh hell." The tears Jennalyn thought she'd suppressed sprang back. Entranced, she walked to the pictures and plucked the one of Sabrina free. She was wearing the same pajamas she'd passed away in.

"He's had that picture for over a year." Michele moved to her side. "Do you know who she is?"

"She was my sister." Jennalyn pressed the photograph to her chest before putting it back in the frame. "I can't believe he brought her home with him."

"He brings them all home with him. Though hers is the only picture I've seen outside his office."

"It's what makes him great at his job." Jennalyn grabbed a paper towel from the roller and dabbed away the tears.

"It's what has him locking himself in this cold apartment while he wears a mask for the outside world."

The statement would have sounded judgmental if Jennalyn hadn't been looking at the concern in Michele's gaze. Ryland's sister was genuinely worried about how involved he was with his patients. She didn't like to see him in pain. She may not fully understand her brother but she loved him.

"For what it's worth, I don't think he always wears a mask outside this apartment."

"Why do say that?" Michele settled onto a bar stool at the island and watched as Jennalyn pulled food from the fridge.

"Your brother is the sweetest, most genuine man, I've ever known. Aside from my own father." Jennalyn opened a cabinet and pulled down a bowl. Below that she opened a drawer and found a fork. "The kind of man he is, the man who worries more about everyone else, isn't a mask."

"You move around like you've been here before. How do you know where he keeps stuff? And if he isn't wearing a mask out there, then why is he so different in here?"

"I guess we share a logic." She didn't want to think too hard about how she just seemed to know where he'd keep things. She cracked some eggs into the bowl and set to work making an omelet. It was basic, but there was a certain comfort in basic. "As for how he is, I think it's more a matter of him allowing the layers of protection to drop when he gets home."

"That's a mask."

"In a way, okay." She heated the stove and an omelet skillet. "But if it is, it's there for his protection."

"What's he need protection from? He's not a doctor anymore. They aren't *his* patients to lose."

"But they are. Every child who walks through the doors of Riley is his." Jennalyn nodded toward the living room where Ryland sat in grief. "Your brother sat with me and my sister while she breathed her last breath. Then he held me until I pulled myself together enough to get home safely. He feels a responsibility for every patient and family member. He's driven to make their lives better."

"He has to know he can't help them all."

"He does know. It doesn't make it easier for him."

"I hate seeing him get so torn up. I never know what to do for him."

Jennalyn poured the eggs into the skillet. "You're doing it."

"I'm not doing anything except sit around and feel helpless."

"Which is how he feels when someone he's grown to care for dies. Knowing that you're here for him though, knowing that you'll pick him up if he falls or just sit here and feel his pain, gives him the strength to start again the next day."

"He's never told me that."

"I would guess it's because he doesn't know how to put it all into words when it's for himself. It's a bit like asking a therapist to diagnose themselves."

"I hadn't thought of it that way." Michele got up and retrieved some plates from another cabinet. She handed one to Jennalyn just as the omelet was ready.

"He's your brother and seeing him in pain pisses you off. It's tough to see past that."

Michele held the plate with a beautiful omelet and studied Jennalyn as she poured more eggs into the skillet for another one.

"Are you a therapist?"

"No. Just an event planner who's dealt with her share of loss." And who would stay with Ryland until he'd pulled himself together enough to face the next day.

Chapter Fifteen

Ryland had hoped to find some time to talk with Jennalyn before their next miracle day. He'd wanted to thank her for tracking him down and cooking for him. Mostly he wanted to thank her for whatever she'd said to Michele, because nothing he'd said over the last several years had made his sister understand him. After an hour with Jennalyn, she seemed to have a new view.

It had made things tremendously easier, because for the first time she hadn't felt the need to watch him as if she thought he was suicidal or something. When he'd pulled himself back in line and told her he was okay, she'd actually believed him. Then she'd gone home without any lectures on how he allowed himself to care too much.

Whatever Jennalyn had said to cause the shift in Michele had simplified his life. Then she'd complicated it again, though he hadn't realized it at the time.

She'd stayed with him through the night, left after cooking him breakfast and then they'd played phone tag for the last two days. He hadn't been able to talk to her. To see her. To touch her. The woman had worked a miracle he hadn't anticipated and she'd been absent since.

In his case, in regards to Jennalyn, absence was not making the heart grow fonder. It was making the heart grow lonelier.

Now, when he should be dealing with the mountain of tasks piled on his desk, he found himself clock watching. There was less than an hour before he would go change for the fun in the snow they had planned. He would meet her, Holly and Holly's aunt at the bridge in Garfield Park.

He wanted to see Holly have a great day. In her ten short years the girl had lost her parents in a plane crash that she'd barely survived and then had been diagnosed with intestinal failure as a result of the trauma she'd sustained in the crash. Moving from Miami to Indiana to live with her aunt had been another shock, but Holly had told Ryland once how much she was looking forward to playing in the snow.

Giving her the chance to build a snowman and have a snowball fight and go down the sledding hill were things he'd been looking forward to. Though the last couple of days his desire to talk to Jennalyn had begun to trump that anticipation.

Then a new idea occurred to him. He would teach Holly all about snowball fights. And before it was over he would take Jennalyn to the ground.

"That's a downright wicked smile." Blanche, his secretary, set more papers on Ryland's desk. "I pity whoever it's geared for. Or should she be envied?"

"I'm sure I don't know what you're talking about."

"I believe I'm talking about whatever plans you have for today and the lovely Jennalyn James."

"Just some fun and games in the snow."

"Sure. Did your lady find you the other night?"

"She did. Are you the one who told her where I live?"

"Nope. I know how to protect your privacy. Though it doesn't seem to bother you as much as I'd have thought it would that she tracked you down."

He shrugged. "She's not asking for anything I'm not giving willingly."

"I like that she's not trying to use you for your position or money." Blanche picked up a stack of files he'd already made it through. "Do me a favor and keep your clothes on until you're inside."

"Blanche!"

"We can't afford for you to catch pneumonia. This hospital can't run itself."

He laughed. "You and I both know the board wouldn't waste any time replacing me."

"Maybe they would fill the vacant position. But no one will ever replace you."

"You're sweet, Blanche. I promise I will not do anything you wouldn't do."

"Then we're in real trouble." She winked and headed to the door. "I've done more wicked things than you can imagine."

Ryland blinked at the back of the woman he'd come to think of as a favorite aunt. The idea of her misbehaving was almost as disturbing as the idea of her misbehaving sexually. A shiver shook him. Reaching for a file, he prayed that work would dislodge the images leaping into his mind.

He was still suffering images of Blanche when he approached the bridge in Garfield Park. Jennalyn was already there, standing with her hands on the black rail, watching Holly and her aunt make snow angels. Dressed in a hot-pink coat and coordinating hat, Holly was a splash of vibrancy in a world of white.

Ryland approached quietly, barely crunching the soft snow beneath his feet. He was sure Jennalyn would hear him, but she was absorbed in another world. Unable to keep his hands to himself, he stepped behind her, placed his hands on her hips and kissed her jaw just above her scarf.

She jumped, but then settled just as quickly. "Hey."

"I missed you."

"You've been in meetings."

"So have you it seems."

"We have a lot of new clients demanding appointments. It's nice."

"You deserve the success you're finding."

"I wouldn't have found it without you."

"I saw the event you put together at the zoo. I had nothing to do with what is coming your way."

She turned in his arms and leaned against the rail. Looking up at him, she studied him with her brown eyes that saw too deeply at times. "How are you?"

"I'm good." He kissed her. He'd intended it to be a light brush against her lips, but the moment he tasted her, felt her warmth, he was helpless to pull away. He deepened the kiss, moving as close as their winter layers would allow.

She hummed and returned his kiss. She awakened his desire in ways that had new images replacing those of Blanche. When she pulled away, he missed her instantly.

"You're right. You're good."

"Did I mention I missed you?"

"Yes. And you make it sound dangerous the way you say it."

"Danger can be fun." Or disastrous if the fun didn't go the way he wanted. He was seriously falling for her, though he doubted she was ready to feel the same.

"Maybe." She narrowed her gaze. "But not here. Not now."

"Right." He traced a finger along her cheek, smiling. "Besides, Blanche made me promise to keep my clothes on in the snow."

"I'm sure I don't want to know why that came up between you two."

"You're why. She thinks I have a *thing* for you."

"Yeah, still not sure I want to know."

"Or maybe you just don't like the idea of us talking about you."

"No maybe. I don't like being talked about."

"I'll keep that in mind." He gave her a last kiss and pulled away. "For now, we have plans to play in the snow."

He grabbed her hand and tugged her into a run toward Holly and her Aunt Stacy. The freshness of the cold air whipped through him, invigorating and freeing. He was laughing when they rounded the top of the hill. He sped up, a little too fast. At the edge of the hill he tugged her hand again. They lost their balance and went tumbling down the hill.

Roll after roll they collected snow until they stopped at the bottom of the hill in a tangle of arms and legs. Ryland pushed up on his elbows, raising himself off her. The laughter rumbling through him halted at the first look of Jennalyn covered in snow.

"I had a vision of you beneath me in the snow."

She smacked his shoulder. "Ryland."

"I'll admit this wasn't exactly how I envisioned it, but I'm not arguing."

"Ugh. You're such a man." She shoved him aside and climbed to her feet. He didn't miss the fact that she was laughing, or that it was a genuine laugh that reached the depths of her soul if the blush on her cheeks and the twinkle in her eyes were any indication.

"Mr. Ryland. Ms. Jennalyn," Holly called from the hill above them. "Are you okay?"

"We're fine." He stood and offered a hand to assist Jennalyn up. "Are you ready to make a snowman?"

"I want to go sledding. But not like you do."

"I'm surrounded by women with smart mouths."

"Today was your idea." Jennalyn patted him on the arm and trudged up the hill a little ahead of him. "And remember this little tumble when we get to the snowball portion of things."

"I'll remember." The snowball fight was the portion he'd been looking most forward to.

Jennalyn poured hot chocolate from the thermos she'd brought along and passed a Styrofoam cup to Stacy. "Holly seems to be adjusting pretty well to life in the cold."

"She's always been a go-with-the-flow kind of girl. Totally opposite of me." Stacy pocketed the camera she'd been taking pictures with while Holly and Ryland wrapped up their snowball fight. "She keeps me grounded while reminding me it's okay to have fun."

A soft chuckle, more of a resigned sigh than a laugh, escaped without thought. "My little sister was that way. No matter how caught up I got in the role of adulthood she helped bring me back to the fun side every time I was with her."

Stacy nodded her head toward Ryland, who was ducking behind a barricade he'd built from snow. "It seems you have someone new to do that for you now."

"He's just a friend." She shook her head, rejecting Stacy's

claim. The business that she was still getting the hang of running was exploding. She was just learning how to survive without her family and feel a semblance of happiness. She was not ready to take on a relationship with a man. Even a man as great as Ryland.

"I wish I had a friend who looked at me the way he looks at you." Stacy strolled away to join Holly and Ryland, leaving Jennalyn to her thoughts.

Christmas was a week away. They had two days of miracles left before the final Christmas Eve party. After that she would have no reason to see Ryland regularly. They would both return to their respective lives. Nothing said she couldn't enjoy his company while they were still working together, because while she wasn't interested in a relationship, she enjoyed being with him.

"Hey." Ryland snapped once, loud, in front of her. "Holly's tired and wants to head home."

"Oh. Okay." Jennalyn capped the thermos she'd been holding, not thinking about the cold getting inside. "Sure."

"You all right?"

"Yep." She nodded firmly. "Distracted, but good."

She remained distracted while they said good-bye to Holly and Stacy. Even when Ryland kissed her good-bye, she was distracted. She sat in the parking lot until the car had warmed enough that she began tugging at the scarf because breathing became difficult. One thought commanded her attention.

Ryland.

He had gone back to his office to work; she should do the same. She certainly had enough paperwork, but her mind wouldn't settle on anything other than the image of Ryland poised above her in the snow.

Danger can be fun.

Was it wrong that she wanted to taste his kind of danger? That she wanted his kind of fun? She wanted him to the point that she felt his body against hers. Smelled him. Tasted him.

He'd tied her up, shown her a passion that ran so deep inside she'd barely recognized it as her own. With no memory of making the trip, she pulled into a parking spot near the hospital. It was late. The administrative staff would be gone, or extremely thin. Holding her coat closed at her throat, she headed inside, intent on one destination.

In the hall, she passed a red wagon. She paused to check the license plate. As always it was a painful relief that it wasn't Sabrina's. And like every other time she wondered what it would feel like to actually see Sabrina's wagon.

Shaking it off, pulling thoughts of Ryland to the forefront of her mind, she pushed forward. The outer office where Blanche worked was dark except the light shining in from Ryland's inner office. Jennalyn closed the door behind her and locked it.

Crossing the thick carpet, she expected to feel like an intruder. She didn't. She felt strong and confident. The bravery she needed to go after a man was something that had been missing since Kris walked. Grinning, she relished the return of the feeling.

Ryland sat behind his desk with his shirt sleeves rolled up and his tie abandoned to the couch along with the outer clothes he'd worn to play in the snow. Thin, wire-rimmed glasses perched on his nose as he read a file and made notes. Arousal snapped at her spine, radiated down.

"I had no idea you wore glasses."

"Jennalyn." His head shot up. His eyes widened. "What are you doing here?"

"I missed you." She whispered it, much like he had on the

bridge, and closed and locked his door. She was feeling brave, but that didn't mean she wanted to put on a show if the cleaning crew or someone else entered the outer office.

"I see." He set his pen on top of the folder and rolled his chair back.

"You don't have a late-night meeting or anything, do you?" She dropped her coat to the floor as she walked slowly across the room. Her sweater followed as she stepped free of her boots on the move. Then her pants, and all she had on were her bra and panties as she rounded his desk.

"If I did I wouldn't care." His modulated tone had a hint of laughter. He raised his eyebrow and watched her without blinking.

"I don't suppose you have condoms in this office somewhere?"

"Actually, I've gone back to carrying a couple in my wallet." He rolled farther away from his desk and held his hands out to her.

She linked her fingers with his and climbed onto his lap, straddling him. "You were a Boy Scout, weren't you?"

"Yeah, but I think you could reverse all the training except being prepared."

"You tempt me to try." Rolling her hips, she rubbed herself over him, loving the sensation of their clothes and bodies creating friction. She worked his buttons loose, rolling her hips again. She grew wet and tight against him, nearing the precipice when they were nowhere near naked enough.

"Honey, you don't have to try. I was ready to abandon all responsibility the instant you walked in." Ryland moved his hands to her ass, held her as he stood. Setting her on the desk, he moved away just enough to shuck his pants and underwear and pull the condom from his wallet.

174

She wiggled out of her panties. "Are you always persuaded so easily?"

"Only with you." Sheathing himself in the rubber, he leaned in and kissed her.

His hunger fed her own and awakened deeper longings. Everything about Ryland excited her. His touches, his kisses, reached the darkest corners of her soul. He lit her up and showed her the stars.

Lifting her again, he sat back in his chair so she was again straddling him. Their first time he'd taken control. The next time they'd met as equals. This time he was allowing her to set the pace.

She wanted the pace to be fast.

Bracing her hands on his shoulders, she raised herself a little, adjusted her feet for balance and then sank onto the length of him. The early grip of orgasm screamed through her, blinded her momentarily.

Instinct and the familiarity with his body drove her to a steady cadence. The initial shock of him entering her subsided a fraction, but only enough to keep her from erupting instantly. Each time she rose and fell, easing off him and then taking him deep again, she carried herself closer to that orgasmic point.

Ryland's breaths grew jagged and rushed. Sweat dotted his brow. He bit his bottom lip and dug his head into the top of his chair.

Two more thrusts and they were both flying over the cliff. Heat swarmed, cocooning them. Tension throbbed and then eased in a rushing release.

Ryland was fun. And dangerous.

Chapter Sixteen

A tuxedo-clad, top-hat-wearing carriage driver guided the black draft horse with four white socks to the curb as they exited The Oceanaire Seafood Room. The subtle glow of clear lights lining the rail and canopy of the white carriage bathed the royal purple upholstery in softness. Any other time of the year Ryland would say the mood of a carriage ride was suited for a man trying to seduce a woman. He'd never wanted to put that much effort into a seduction, but in late December, with the wreath on the front of the carriage and small poinsettia blooms on the horse's bridle, and with Jennalyn at his side, he found himself wishing they were alone. He found himself wishing for a Christmas seduction.

The night wasn't for him and Jennalyn, though. They were together for Preston, the nearly six-foot-tall fourteen-year-old who had beaten Ryland to every door all evening. Jennalyn hadn't even lifted a hand to pull her own chair out before or after dinner.

While Ryland would like to be the one holding Jennalyn's doors, the boy's courtesy was refreshing in today's society. That he'd survived a lung transplant had gotten him on Ryland's list of possible miracle recipients. It was the things the staff had said about him, the way he treated others, always thinking of how his actions impacted those around him, that had made giving him a special night a treat.

Ryland handed his ticket to the valet and smiled at the carriage driver who moved to help a couple into their chosen ride. If their next stop were closer, he would have suggested hiring a carriage, but two and a half hours in the chilled night air would be a little much.

"Your car, sir."

Ryland pulled a five from his pocket and passed it to the valet. As expected, by the time he turned to open the door for Jennalyn, Preston was there. He took her fingers in his and offered her balance as she slid into the front seat.

When they were all settled in the car's growing warmth, Ryland headed toward their next stop. The Christmas lights on the Circle reflected off windows and cars, bouncing their cheer everywhere. Preston may be a teenager, but he still looked out the windows, trying to take it all in.

Unlike the night of the movie, the light strands that stretched from the top of the monument to the ground to create a tree were shining. It was better than any Christmas tree the city could have erected, more powerful in the way the lights formed a shield of brightness around the memorial. For the month of December, the heroes being honored on the Circle shone unlike any other time.

Jennalyn turned in her seat to see Preston better. "I understand you're in the National Junior Honor Society."

"Yes, ma'am."

"You must have had to work hard to keep your grades up enough to earn that honor. More than most kids because of the school you missed."

"I did, but now that I'm able to participate more it was worth it."

"Your mom was telling me that you've been looking for some volunteer work," Ryland injected.

"Yeah. I'd really like to help out at the hospital, but my doctors think that since I've gone back to school that it's best if I choose someplace a little less contagious for a while longer."

"Have you given thought to what else you would like to do for hours?" Jennalyn asked, as if she wanted to help Preston find the perfect fit.

"I've spent some time in a nursing home, reading and playing cards with some of the residents. I've done some database entry for my dad's office." He shrugged as only a teenager could. It was half acceptance and half defiance. His pride in what he was doing was obvious though. So was his desire for his life to matter.

Ryland only partially registered the lights in the windows of the buildings they were passing. One building had covered some windows in green so that when the lights inside were on it looked like a giant Christmas tree. "You said you want to study astronomy when you go to college."

"I do. I'm fascinated by what we could one day learn by studying the things beyond our own atmosphere."

Glancing in the rearview mirror, hoping to see Preston's face when he figured out where they were headed, Ryland turned into the main entrance of Butler University and headed toward Holcomb Observatory and Planetarium.

Preston sat a little straighter in the seat. "Where are we going?"

The excitement in his voice even as he asked the question confirmed his suspicion. Ryland grinned as he said, "Given your fascination with astronomy, we thought you would enjoy a private evening at the planetarium."

"They'll be opening the observatory for you," Jennalyn

added.

"Seriously?" Preston scooted forward on the seat, ready to burst out of the car before they even stopped. His voice became as animated as his face as they neared the building. "This is beast! I've been here on public tours, but have never actually gotten to look through the telescope."

As they pulled up outside, a Chinese man stepped through the doors and waited on the porch. Ryland lifted a hand in greeting.

Preston's jaw dropped. "That's Dr. Sun."

"He's expecting you."

"One of the head professors is expecting me?"

"Yes."

The moment Ryland eased the car to a stop, Preston pushed open his door and jumped out. Ryland turned off the car and smiled at Jennalyn.

"It seems you've been replaced as his crush." He couldn't help laughing.

She was smiling too as she watched Preston stare up at the building before him. "You think it's funny?"

"Yes." Ryland turned off the engine and went to open her door. Holding her hand, he kissed her cheek. "I would never be so fickle in my affection for you."

"Fickle or not, he holds a certain appeal."

"Jailbait. Yuck."

"Ugh. Gutter. Gutter, Ryland. As if I would consider a teenager." She backhanded him in the stomach.

"I guess it's good that you wouldn't." He nodded toward Preston and Dr. Sun. "You don't exist in this world for him."

Smiling, she slid an arm around Ryland's waist and walked

toward the planetarium with him. "This could be the best outing."

"Certainly the most impactful." If Preston worked the night right, he wouldn't just have a great time. He could easily find himself with a volunteer position that would earn him hours for NJHS and potentially morph into something more lasting.

They followed Dr. Sun and Preston to the telescope in the observatory. Neither Ryland nor Jennalyn interjected themselves into the conversation between Preston and a man he obviously idolized.

"Preston," Dr. Sun pointed to the telescope. "Can you tell me what part of the sky and which constellation is in view right now?"

Preston glanced in the scope and then turned back to Dr. Sun. "We're facing north, so the constellations we should see include Perseus, Cassiopeia, Drago, Ursas Minor and Major, and Andromeda. There are others, of course, but those are probably some of the more famous ones."

Preston looked through the telescope again and considered for a moment. "I'm pretty sure this is Andromeda, the Chained Princess."

"Very good," Dr. Sun praised him. "Perhaps Mr. Davids or Ms. James would like a look."

"Of course." Preston stepped back and held a hand out for Jennalyn. The chivalrous young man was returning with the first blast of excitement having abated.

When Jennalyn was in position, Preston told her exactly what she was looking for. "Do you see her?"

"I do."

"That bright star at the head of her is Alpha Andromedae." Dr. Sun's voice took on a teaching tone that soothed and informed. "That is the brightest star of Andromeda."

"Down a little and to the left a little is another cluster of stars." Ryland stepped up and spoke low. "One of those stars has been named Sabrina."

Jennalyn straightened and spun. "What?"

"Sabrina was a princess to you. I wanted to somehow show you that she's still with you. She's watching you from the heavens."

Jennalyn's eyes watered with what Ryland hoped were happy tears.

"Dude. Sabrina James was your little sister?" Preston asked.

"Yes." Jennalyn turned toward Preston with more surprise lighting her face. "Did you know her?"

"I met her in the hospital library a few times. She found me reading about stars and their planets and told me that it was crazy to believe mythical gods put people in the sky." Preston laughed at something only he was privy to. "Her theory was that the fairies put them there."

"She was needling you." Jennalyn laughed a laugh that was lighter in mood than Ryland would have thought possible in the moment. "She loved to challenge people who made their opinions and thoughts well known. She always went for the shock factor."

"Mr. Davids," Preston turned to Ryland, "that is officially the coolest present ever. Does it come with a certificate too?"

Jennalyn's smile grew wider. There was no sadness showing on her face. Only happiness, and it thrilled Ryland that he'd been the one to put it there. "It is a pretty cool present, Ryland."

"I'm glad you like it. And it does come with a certificate, as well as a map that shows exactly which star is Sabrina's."

"I spoke with Mr. Davids earlier today." Dr. Sun led them to one of the smaller telescopes. "This is already set to show you Sabrina's star."

"I've said it before. I'll say it again. You're a sweet man." Jennalyn kissed Ryland on the cheek. She turned and kissed Preston on his cheek. "And thank you for remembering Sabrina."

"She was adorable. She is unforgettable." He grinned. "And she would love having a star named after her."

Jennalyn checked the list she'd been double-checking as they loaded the gifts into the new company van. "Chrissy, where are the iPods? We haven't loaded those."

"I've got them here." Chrissy kicked the office door closed behind her and carried a large box to the van. "Are we missing anything else?"

"The stuffed animals were being delivered directly to the hospital to Child Life. We should be set." The idea of missing a kiddo, or of running out of age-appropriate toys wasn't acceptable. The kids who were spending the week of Christmas in the hospital deserved something special.

Jennalyn was still stressing that they'd miss someone when they pulled up to the hospital's loading docks. Climbing out of the van, she headed into the mail receiving area where they would stage their deliveries.

A group of volunteers came to attention when she stepped inside. The firefighters and EMTs from Zack's station, Preston and Gavin, several of the family members who'd helped decorate the Ronald McDonald House. They had lined up carts, enough for six for each floor, and were ready to take instructions.

Child Life was there with a list of all the patients, their room numbers and ages. After a few small bumps, they had the van unloaded and the carts were being stocked with the appropriate toys in accordance with where the cart would go.

The work kept Jennalyn distracted from where she was until the group pushed through the double doors and they entered the hospital halls. Rubber soled shoes slapped linoleum floors. Monitors beeped. Children and adults talked or laughed or cried.

Emotions slapped Jennalyn, had her stumbling in her steps. She'd loved the idea of delivering gifts to the kids in their rooms, but now that the time had come she wasn't sure she could. She backed up two steps, retreating toward the mailroom. The van.

"Oh good." Ryland's voice cut through the fog clouding her mind. "You guys are ready."

He closed the distance between them and smiled to the director of Child Life while talking to Jennalyn. "Jennalyn, we have your floor picked out."

Gently bulldozing her toward the elevator, he took her hand and moved her away from the exit. She vaguely noticed that everyone hung back, giving them privacy on the elevator. The floor number he pushed didn't register, not that it would matter. There would be patients in pain. Parents in tears.

"Ryland, I can't do this," she whispered through the panic gripping her throat. She'd barely handled the hospital visits when she'd stayed in the public areas. He was dragging her into the heart of agony. "I can't be here."

"Trust me."

"I can't. I can't forget the sounds of loss that permeate these halls. I can't forget the tears or the crushing weight of

183

death." She trembled as the elevator rose. "I can't be here."

"JJ." He took her in his arms and hugged her. "I figured you would feel that way, but I also know you want to make these kids happy."

"I'm okay knowing someone else gave them the gifts."

"I can't allow you to hide out during all of this." He kissed her head. "For that reason, I picked a floor where you don't have to worry about those things."

"It's a children's hospital. That's always a worry."

"You may hear some tears or complaints of pain. But we're going to the orthopedic floor. The kids there have had surgeries to correct their joints and spines."

She didn't remind him that bone tumors were a big part of bone issues. Instead, she latched on to the idea that they were going to one of the least fatal floors in the place. Maybe she could make it through the day.

The doors chimed open. They stepped into a nurse's station. Her hands shook as she fidgeted with the ring Ryland had given her, but her heart remained fairly steady.

The smells of medicine and disinfectants mixed with coffee and hospital food in a cacophony of misery. She'd always hated the smell of hospitals. She'd grown to especially hate it over her stay with Sabrina.

"Jennalyn. Ryland." Rhea, the too-perky nurse who didn't seem to know when to back off, rounded the desk. "Are you two going to be handing out the gifts on our floor?"

"Some of them," Ryland answered, steering Jennalyn in the opposite direction.

"I'm not sure what's greater. The gifts or that you two are getting together." Rhea, as usual, was undeterred. She followed them into the sitting area where a couple of kids played. "You're perfect for each other. You make great partners."

A dad walked in pulling a red wagon.

"We're not..." Jennalyn's argument died on her lips. On the back of the wagon, in bold black letters, was Sabrina's name.

Sorrow stabbed, deep and sharp. Tears burned her eyes. Buzzing obliterated her hearing. She stumbled. Swayed.

Ryland caught her and helped her to the closest chair. Jennalyn's eyes stayed locked on the wagon and the smiling girl sitting inside it. She had brown hair and a smile so bright that it reminded Jennalyn of Sabrina.

Her mind jumped back to the night she'd surprised Sabrina with the wagon ride. They'd had so much fun, laughed so hard. It had been the last time she'd had that much fun with her sister.

I love you, JJ. Sabrina's voice was a whispering hope in her head. *Ryland is perfect for you.*

"I'm so sorry." Ryland wrapped an arm around her shoulder. He placed his other hand on her knee, massaged. "I had no idea that was up here."

"I can't do this. I can't be here." Shaking her head, staring at the red wagon she'd wanted desperately to see but now wished she hadn't, she rose. "I can't do any of this. Chrissy will help you finish today and the closing party."

Standing before the elevator, not remembering walking there, she jabbed the down button. The only clear thought was escape. She had to get away from the hospital, from the kids, the smells, the memories.

Pressure whirled around her as if she was caught in a vortex of darkness. She'd have been fine if they'd only run into Rhea or if they'd only seen the wagon. The two together along with the memory of what Sabrina wanted for her and Ryland,

and what she thought she might be feeling for him, pushed Jennalyn to her break.

The vortex of pressure spun faster.

Squeezed tighter.

Grew darker.

Then, there was only dizzying darkness.

Ryland caught Jennalyn as she began to fall. Fear had him carrying her unconscious body as he tracked Chrissy down to get Jennalyn's purse and house keys from their van. Then he carried Jennalyn to his car and drove her home.

She moved in and out of unconsciousness the whole time, mumbling about the wagon, Rhea, the expectations. When she became aware of her surroundings for a moment she would clutch her head and faint again. It was as if the pain of her memories was too much to stand, but there was more to whatever was going on with her than seeing the wagon. Sure, that was a big part of it, but the shift didn't make sense. She'd been handling all the events well, even those at the hospital.

A couple of times he'd noticed a hitch in her stride, but she'd moved past it and done what she needed. Something more happened at the hospital. Something he didn't know about because it had been in her mind.

He could help with things he knew about, like the wagon, but not an issue he couldn't identify. The helplessness restricted his ability to breathe easily.

In her driveway, he turned off the car and turned to her. "Jennalyn. You're home."

She simply sat beside him with her eyes closed and her breathing steady. She could be asleep, but he knew better. She wasn't relaxed enough to rest.

He grabbed her purse and pulled out her key. After pulling her from the car, he carried her toward the front door. The cold air hitting her face brought her to awareness.

"Where am I?"

"Home." Shifting her in his arms, doubtful that she was strong enough to stand alone just yet, he unlocked the door and carried her to the couch. "You fainted. A couple of times."

Curling into the corner, she held her head like it throbbed. "I'm sorry I pulled you away from the gift deliveries."

"Don't be." Moving easily into caregiver mode, he stripped her of her coat and shoes. After getting her robe from her bedroom closet, he helped her slip into it, assuming that it would give her a level of comfort.

He turned on the lights to her tree, but she begged him to turn them off. He didn't like the idea of her sitting in the dark, but she winced every time he turned something on. She refused to eat, but he set a bowl of trail mix at her side.

She'd shrunk back into the grief of losing her family. The wound had been scraped open at the sight of Sabrina's wagon, and nothing he did tonight would ease her pain. Sitting at her side, bathed again in the feeling of helplessness, Ryland kissed her temple. "I'm sorry you're hurting again, JJ."

She swiped at a tear, but said nothing.

"Do you want me to stay?"

Nothing.

He sighed and kissed her again. "Promise you will call if you need me."

Still nothing. Her silence and blank stare gave him no opening. She'd shut herself off from the world. She needed space to find her way back, to remember all that she'd begun embracing over the last month. This time though he wasn't giving her a year. And he wasn't relying on DVDs of her sister to reinforce reality.

"I'll be back soon."

Chapter Seventeen

"Yes. Eleven tables. Ten chairs at each." Jennalyn skimmed her notes, making sure she didn't miss anything on the closing event for A Month of Miracles. "White tablecloths with a smaller red one over them."

"Yes, Ms. James."

"They need to be delivered no later than five."

"They'll be there," the manager assured her.

"Let's not have a repeat of the last time." She was taking a chance on the table company she'd used for the zoo's fundraiser. If they messed up the order this time, she would find a new vendor.

After thanking the manager for the assurances things would run smoothly, she clicked to line two and dialed the number for the florist.

"Andrew's Florists. Let us freshen your day."

"This is Jennalyn James. I was calling to confirm the wreaths for the Christmas Eve party at the zoo."

"Yes, ma'am. We're putting the final touches on them. The larger wreath for the door is finished."

"Excellent." She'd approached them for something custom, but when she'd seen the holiday bridal wreath, she'd chosen it minus the satin sash for carrying. The small wreaths would sit on each table with a bear in the circle. "And the stepping stones?"

"We have received them with the customized messages."

"You have us down for delivery at five thirty?"

"We do. It's going to be an amazing evening. People are going to love the stones."

"Perfect." She swallowed. Emotion had nearly strangled her while she'd been searching for quotes to put on stepping stones. They'd celebrated ten children through the month. Each child would take home a stepping stone, but the one that had touched her the most had said "The soul is healed by being with children." It was from a nineteenth-century Russian novelist, but she'd wanted the words to be true.

She'd thought she was healing, that she was doing okay around the kids. The last trip to the hospital had been overwhelming and painful, but it hadn't been the place or the kids that sent her into a panic. The idea that people saw her and Ryland as a committed couple had been too much.

She'd come to the realization that it wasn't a relationship she didn't have time for. A relationship with Ryland was one she didn't have the heart for. She wasn't strong enough to be involved with a man who took his work home with him the way Ryland did. Every time he got sad over the loss of a patient she would be reminded of Sabrina. She needed more distance than that if she hoped to heal.

Shaking off the threatening melancholy, knowing that if she allowed it purchase she would be huddled in a corner with her robe again, she made her next call to the DJ.

Thirty minutes later she'd finalized the song list. She'd carefully considered the people she'd met during the outings with Ryland and worked to pick songs that would suit everyone. During dinner, they would play softer music that allowed for conversation. After dinner, the tone would shift to songs with a great beat for dancing.

They would play a range of things from line dances to funny kid songs, like the chicken dance, to oldies and of course Christmas carols. Ryland had asked for an evening that would have people enjoying themselves. She was going to give him an unforgettable party.

She was halfway through dialing the next number when Chrissy walked in and plopped herself in the chair across the desk. "Do you really intend to skip this party?"

"Did Ryland put you up to this?" He'd called a few times. She hadn't called him back.

"No. Answer my question."

"Yes. I really plan on skipping the party."

"But you've worked so hard to put it all together. You've gotten to know the people who are going to be there."

"I have to cut things off, Chrissy." She'd barely pulled herself together that morning to make it to the office. She'd hurt in the depths of every muscle, like she had after losing her family. The loss was different this time. Not grief-worthy but still painful like a part of her had been cut out.

Now, just as then, the only thing that pushed her out the door in the morning was the realization that her staff counted on her. If she crumbled, the business would crumble. If the business crumbled she'd be leaving people without jobs. She'd be disgracing the wishes of her parents.

"Not before you finish the job you started. Jennalyn, these people think of you as much as they do Ryland when they think of A Month of Miracles."

"I'm not in a mood to party, Chrissy."

"You're not even going to the site to help set up."

"I trust you to oversee the details." As raw as she was, she couldn't make another trip to the zoo. She would be drawn to the dome, and the memories would attack.

"What if I refuse?"

"You won't. You need the bonus you'll get from the extra work."

"Money isn't everything, you know?"

"I know. I also know that you won't let the kids or their families down."

"We can't afford to have two stubborn cowards in this company, Jennalyn."

"You're not a coward."

"Apparently I am because I'm not turning down the money to make you follow through on the party." Chrissy shook her head slowly. The next time she spoke it was with a quiet resolution. "Your parents and Sabrina would be disappointed in you."

Jennalyn flinched.

Chrissy plopped a box on her desk and marched out.

Jennalyn eyed the box for several minutes before reaching for it. The shiny red wrapping with the silver bow looked harmless enough. Some instinct told her the gift wasn't harmless.

Pulling the small card from beneath the crisscrossed ribbon, she unfolded the paper.

I was going to give this to you after we delivered the last gift yesterday, but...

Crystal geodes are crystal-filled caves of power. It's said if you whisper your heart's dream into them that magic will help it come true. I have a matching geode. Let's see if magic is real.

Ryland

Lifting the lid, she found herself looking at a gorgeous geode. White and bumpy on the outside, its cut side had been polished smooth. The inside had varying shades of white and ivory rings circling it. The inside crystals were mostly white with black flecks sprinkled throughout. More flecks of bright white sparked throughout, winking at her like the clear lights on her tree.

Sabrina would have loved it. She'd have gone on and on about its beauty. Then she'd have made up some crazy and likely hysterical story about how the fairies created it. She'd really loved fairies.

"Talking to a rock isn't going to solve anything." Jennalyn covered the geode and slid the box aside. She had phone calls to make, plans to finalize, or there would only be half a Christmas Eve party.

Over the next three hours she finalized details with the caterer, the baker, Mass Ave Toys who was delivering presents for the attending kids, the tree farm that was taking in a decorated tree, and the zoo.

Through it all her gaze drifted back to the gift Ryland had sent. Each time she shook herself off the trail her thoughts wanted to traverse.

She'd put together the components of what promised to be a rocking party. If she was in the mood for holiday festivities, and if she thought she could see Ryland without making unfulfillable wishes, it was the kind of party she would go to.

Chrissy was more than capable of supervising the staff to get the room transformed with the decorations they had. She would take pictures for the website too.

Jennalyn would miss not seeing with her own eyes how it

all came together, but it wasn't a strong enough drive for her to attend. Her eyes shifted again to the wrapped box. He'd now given her a gift for every outing they'd planned.

What would his last gift have been?

Ryland had gone by Jennalyn's house only to find it dark each time. He'd tried catching her at work, but always missed her. He'd left her voicemails and sent her text messages. She ignored them all. If he claimed to be calling about the party she had Chrissy return his call.

She needed to be at the party for him to deliver his final gift. A more perfect opportunity would never exist.

Damn it, though.

The woman took stubborn, evasive and reclusive to new highs. He didn't know what else to try. Even Chrissy had failed in her attempts to get Jennalyn to the zoo for set up.

"I'm really sorry she isn't coming tonight." Chrissy stepped up, offering him a glass of wine. "She'd have loved it."

"I was sure she'd want to see everyone together. That they'd come to matter enough that she'd have put them before her own sadness."

"What happened at the hospital?" Chrissy asked. "I haven't seen her so guarded since before Sabrina died. Even after Sabrina she was more open than she is right now?"

"She saw the wagon she sponsored. It sent her into a tailspin I'm not sure I can pull her out of."

"No." Chrissy took a drink of her wine and looked around the room. "I don't think that's it."

"Why not?"

"That's too easy. I mean, seeing the wagon would have

194

upset her, but she was doing better with her grief. She could have handled that. She was finding happiness again."

"Then what is wrong with her?" What had he missed between the elevator and the waiting area? "What would send her back into her cave?"

"If I knew that I would've had better luck getting her here."

"You and me both." His shoulders dropped with his mood. Then the door opened to the first family. He straightened himself up, put on the mask his sister accused him of wearing so well, and pretended he was ready to party.

Jennalyn poured a glass of wine and headed into the living room where she'd piled the empty decoration boxes by the tree. Turning on the TV, intent on finding a cheesy Christmas movie to watch while stripping the tree, she bumped the input button.

The screen changed and Sabrina's image was paused from the last time she'd watched a DVD. It had been the one she found the night Ryland had told her about Bria. She'd never finished it because she'd cared more about Ryland.

Sinking onto the couch, she hit play.

"In all seriousness, JJ." Sabrina sobered from whatever she'd been joking about. Jennalyn couldn't remember now. It didn't matter. "What you're going to do with Ryland, the month you'll have, is going to change lives. Some days will hurt, but do me a favor. Be brave enough to see it to the end. Don't run scared if things get hard. Remember what Daddy used to say. Glide. Embrace the moment."

The screen went black. As a parting shot from her sister it was a good one.

Jennalyn sipped her wine. She wasn't sure she knew how

to be brave.

The Chipmunks sang about all the things they wanted for Christmas. Laughter and smiles filled the room as people milled around the cake table and began moving to the dance floor.

It was a great party, but a shadow seemed to muddle the excitement.

The song wrapped up. Chrissy spoke through the microphone. "Are you having fun?"

"Yes!" The chorus of cheers was expected.

"Good." Chrissy grinned. "But there's more fun to be had. Could I get my helper up here?"

Zack moved to where the tree stood by the DJ's booth. They hadn't talked him into wearing a complete Santa suit, but he'd gone for the hat and a bright red sweatshirt emblazoned with *Call me Santa!*

Chrissy smiled at the firefighter she had settled into a steamy romance with. "Rachel, Dawn, Paige, Preston, Holly, Di, Blake, Gavin, Viv and Cooper, will you all come up here?"

The kids made their way to the DJ's stage. Each one of them wore a curious smile. "You've each had a special day where you met my friend Jennalyn," Chrissy said.

They all nodded.

"Well, she put a little something together for you guys tonight, but before we get to that, I want us to do something for her."

"Okay." The agreement was unanimous.

"Ryland and I would like to get a group photo of you guys so we can give it to her as a thank you."

"Okay."

"Awesome."

"It's not enough."

Several other statements came from the kids and their families. Seeing everyone together, witnessing how quickly they'd all found friendship, made breathing difficult and it had tears lodging.

Zack wheeled a red wagon out from behind the tree and began situating the kids for the picture. He put the smaller ones in the wagon. When he stepped back Sabrina's license plate was in the center.

Breathing became impossible.

Then, as quick as a round of flashes, they were finished with the picture.

"Now, to get back to the fun." Chrissy riled the kids up again. "Back to Jennalyn's last surprise for you."

The kids' grins spread.

"Santa Zack," Chrissy winked at Zack, "would you do the honors?"

Zack bent down and picked up a long, skinny present from beneath the tree. Opening a card, he read a name. "Preston."

Preston looked from Chrissy to Ryland to Zack to the crowd in the room. "I don't need anything else."

"I believe that's something you would all say." Chrissy laughed a little. "It's also what makes giving you presents fun."

Zack called the rest of them up one at a time. They all headed back to the line in front of the DJ and waited to open the gifts at once.

Ryland was ready in the front of the group with a camera, not that there would be a shortage of pictures thanks to the families.

The gifts ranged from a massive collection of sandbox tools for Blake to a fairy village for Viv to a high-powered telescope for Preston. Every one of them, from the youngest to the oldest, squealed their delight. Then they moved into a corner of the room free of tables and began setting things up. The older kids helped the younger ones set stuff up. Dads and moms chipped in with aunts, uncles and grandparents sitting in nearby chairs to watch.

Ten families had been touched by A Month of Miracles.

Ten families shared their Christmas.

Ten families voiced the idea of getting together every Christmas Eve.

Unable to watch from the shadowy corner any longer, Jennalyn stepped into the light with tears streaming down her face. She had to look like a horrible mess with a red nose and runny mascara, but she couldn't hide from the kids who'd taught her to have fun again.

Holly saw her first. She quietly rose from the floor and walked over. Jennalyn sank into a nearby chair so she was at the same level as the little girl who'd made snow angels in Garfield Park.

"Thank you, Ms. Jennalyn." She wrapped her little arms around Jennalyn and wrapped her in a strawberry-scented hug. "I really like my Barbies."

"You're welcome."

Her composure was shot, and it wasn't going to be returning any time soon. She looked up from Holly to see that the other kids had gathered around. Behind them, with a proud smile, stood Ryland.

"Jennalyn."

"Guess I couldn't stay away."

"I'm glad." Ryland circled the kids and knelt at her side. "I'd have hated for you to miss getting your last present."

She laughed, feeling more than a little nervous with him on his knee at her side. "I don't think I can handle any more presents from you for a while."

"Well, this is my best chance for this one." He nodded toward the kids. "These guys were right when they said you deserved more than a picture."

"I don't. I was just doing a job."

"You weren't doing a job when you made the toughest decision of your life."

"What?" Confusion mixed with more tears.

"You haven't spent the month with a group of random kids, JJ." Ryland paused, giving her a moment to think. The silence, the gazes looking at her, were shattering blows to the miniscule composure that remained.

"No." The whispered denial contradicted the hope in her heart.

"These kids are the recipients of Sabrina's organs and tissues, with the exception of Cooper. He's still with us because of your generosity and strength because Sabrina's was the body Zack studied. She's the reason he was able to save Cooper. The reason he'll be able to save so many more kids."

Tears fell unchecked. Her nose went from runny to stuffy. Her face was on fire. And her heart... Her heart ached with sorrow and happiness all at once.

Sabrina had requested that her organs be donated to sick kids and that her body go to study. It had been the roughest promise to keep, but seeing the kids who carried a piece of her sister with them, knowing that they all appreciated the gift, healed the biggest pain in her own heart.

She would always miss her baby sister, but Ryland had found a way to show her how profoundly special Sabrina had been. He'd brought her full circle from the moment they were reunited to his reveal.

He'd hired her to make miracles happen, but he'd become her miracle man.

Chapter Eighteen

The sun rose over the zoo as Ryland closed the door behind the last family. He turned back and went to the table where Jennalyn sat.

"It's been forever since I pulled an all-nighter at a party."

"They didn't want to leave because of you." He sank into a chair and propped his head on a hand. He was exhausted in one of the two best possible ways. He was currently too tired for the other best.

She leaned on her hand, mirroring him. "You've known who those kids were. Why didn't you tell me? Did they know who I was?"

"Their parents knew. They asked me about the donor shortly after the surgeries."

"Is that all of them?"

"All that I know of." He took her hand that rested on her lap and ran his thumb over her knuckles.

"How is it possible that they were all patients at Riley? Organs and tissue go all over the place."

"The process is a complicated one. A couple of these kids were at the top of wait lists or others came down to a matching blood type. Mostly, they stayed local because weather made getting the organs anywhere else in time impossible."

"The blizzard."

He nodded. "We're used to snow, but that storm last year nearly closed down the city."

"I hadn't given it any thought. Though I knew these kids were organ recipients it never occurred to me that they would have received Sabrina's."

"Cooper is the only one without a part of Sabrina."

"My family has always talked about wanting to help people. My parents specifically stated several times that they wanted to be donated for their organs and research. I have no idea who they might have saved." She tapped her fingers on her cheek. The ring he gave her danced on her right ring finger. "I was too wrapped up in rearranging my world and taking care of Sabrina to think about it."

"We can reach out to the coordinators to see if they would like to meet you."

"It's been a rough month." She shook her head. "I think I've had my quota of these reunions for awhile."

"JJ." He brought her hand up and kissed her knuckles. "The legacy you passed on, the strength you showed by donating Sabrina's body to medical research, is something that can't be matched."

"I almost didn't do it. I couldn't get past the idea of people cutting into her. What if they didn't show her the right kind of respect?" She went silent, retreating into her thoughts for several moments. "I almost backed out, and now I look at Cooper..."

"Honey, no one would have blamed you if you had made a different choice. In fact, outside of the people who were in this room tonight, you're likely to be judged more harshly for the choice you did make." He kissed her hand again. "There's no way I could have donated Elise for research. Even when I was in medical school, studying pediatrics and wishing we had something more than mannequins to practice on, I knew I wouldn't have made a different choice."

"Sabrina wasn't my daughter, and she was old enough to voice her desire. I couldn't deny her last request." She smiled. "Well, her next-to-last request as it turned out."

"Do you think you can forgive me for keeping secrets and the DVDs?"

"I don't know, Ryland." She sank deeper into her palm. "You kept secrets, you didn't tell me about Sabrina's plans, you gave me gifts with meaning, and you gave me some of my sister back. I'll watch those kids grow and know that they carry Sabrina with them." She squeezed his hand. "I'm not sure you *need* forgiveness, though I do want to see the other set of DVDs."

"They're all yours." He smiled, certain he would win her heart completely before long. "I hated keeping the secrets."

"You gave me Sabrina back, and so much more." She pulled his hand to her, pressed a kiss into his palm. "Holding anything against you would be impossible."

"Can I tell you something else you may not be ready to hear?"

"Not if you get on your knee again."

"No proposal." The idea had occurred to him the moment he took a knee before her. And every time he looked at the ring on her right ring finger he'd seen the proposal as it would play out. Eventually.

"Then shoot."

"I'm falling in love with you." He shrugged. "Actually, I'm pretty sure I've fallen all the way. I don't like the days when I don't see or talk to you."

"Ryland."

He silenced her with a kiss. When he pulled back, he met her gaze. "I don't want you to say you don't feel the same. And I don't want you to say you do if you don't."

"Then what do you want?"

"For the moment, I want you to accept that I love you. And I want you to spend the day with me." A yawn popped his jaw. "After a nap."

"It's Christmas."

"Yes. And I am going to my parents' tonight for presents and dinner. I want you to come with me."

"I..." She shook her head, straightening in the chair. It was another retreat. "I can't... I'm not ready for a big family Christmas. I would feel like I needed to do some last-minute shopping."

"We're not a big family. Or a loud one. And trust me when I say that you've already given my family the best gift possible."

Her eyebrows scrunched together.

"You've given me a reason to do something other than work. You helped Michele understand my job, though I'm not sure how. You've made me happy, JJ. My family wouldn't want any more than that."

"Right. So no pressure for the first-time guest."

"None." He ignored her sarcasm, taking the statement as her agreement to spend the day with him. Maybe, if he diagnosed their relationship correctly, he would have a ring on her finger by next Christmas.

He had no doubt she would plan one hell of a wedding. And after this month, she had a considerable crew to fill her side of a church.

The trip to Carmel, to Ryland's family home, was just over thirty minutes. In the grand scheme of things that wasn't long. For a woman who just the day before had been ready to quit Christmas and sink into her loneliness, it was an eternity.

Ryland had told her he loved her. Then he'd taken her to his apartment where they'd crashed into a coma-like sleep. When she finally woke up, it was to Ryland's gentle touches and more whispers of his love. It was all very idyllic.

"Thank you for coming with me today." Ryland took her hand in his and kissed her knuckles. He'd been doing that a lot, as if he worried if he stopped showering her with affection she might bolt.

The suffocating feeling she'd had in the hospital when she'd seen Sabrina's wagon closed in. Too much emotion and possibilities of how he saw things taking shape between them built too quickly. "I changed my mind."

"My dad is going to love you."

"I can't do the family thing this year."

"My mom too for that matter."

"It's too soon."

"Michele already adores you."

"Take me back."

"Did I mention she's bringing a boyfriend?" Ryland talked over her, ignoring her pleas. "He's a doctor. Mom thinks an engagement is forthcoming." He turned into a neighborhood that was straight from a greeting card.

Tall, snow-covered trees lined the street and filled the yards. It wasn't much different from the neighborhood she lived in, only hers was a little smaller in scale. Neighbors would know each other. They would have community cook outs and all the kids would attend each other's birthday parties. It was everything she'd imagined having for herself one day.

"That's nice."

"Not really. The guy's a player with an overinflated God complex."

Sounded like her ex. "Michele's smart. She'll figure it out."

"She's been with him a year and a half." Ryland shook his head as he pulled into the doublewide driveway. "I'm beginning to wonder."

Several large windows ran across the front of the house, upstairs and down. In the main window facing the street, a huge tree winked with clear lights. With subtle green paint and a rough rock exterior, the home blended beautifully into the surrounding nature. Jennalyn could imagine stepping outside on a crisp fall morning, coffee in hand, to find a couple of grazing deer.

The home was as welcoming as the man who'd grown up in it. Her anxiety rose and fell with anticipation and worry. She suspected she would like the people waiting inside as much as she'd liked Michele. The more she liked Ryland's family the more difficult it would be to accept moving on without him when he discovered there was someone better than her.

"Can you get the door?" Ryland asked as they went up the steps to the entrance. His arms were full of the gifts.

She nodded and opened the door. Closing it behind him, she took a bracing breath. When she turned toward the living room, she was struck by the definition of hearth and home.

Vaulted ceilings with white beams, walls a green so soft it almost wasn't green and furniture that suited moods more than any specific theme. The light from outside flooded in from the large windows at the front, back and side of the room.

A large fireplace of the same rock that covered the outside of the house was the focal point of the room. A rustic beam served as the mantle, with four mismatched stockings dangling from hooks. Mom. Dad. Ryland. Michele. Evergreen garland ran along the mantle with silly reindeer playing around it. Santa and Mrs. Claus, probably three-feet high, stood sentry on either side of the flickering fire.

The centerpiece on the table and the homemade ornaments on the tree added to the impression. And then the scents hit her. Pumpkin. Cinnamon. Ham. Sweet potatoes. It was everything she remembered from Christmas with her parents. Her heart clutched at the memory.

Ryland placed the gifts by the tree and then returned to Jennalyn with his hands extended. "Your coat, m'lady."

She laughed as she handed over her coat, gloves, scarf and hat. "Do visits home always make you behave so... I'm not sure what that is."

"Silly? Yes," a woman said from just inside the room. "Ryland, come introduce your lady."

He tossed Jennalyn's coat over the staircase banister, took her hand and then tugged her into the living room. "Mom, this is Jennalyn. Jennalyn, my mom, Ellen."

Ellen skipped the tradition of a handshake. She pulled Jennalyn into a hug, snug in the comfort it gave. "It's lovely to have you with us. Ryland, put the coats away and come to the kitchen. Michele and her beau are here."

Jennalyn looked over her shoulder, watching Ryland while his mother led her away. His smile told her that he wouldn't rush to her rescue. Or that it wouldn't do him any good to try because Ellen Davids was definitely the neck that turned all the heads in the family.

Jennalyn turned away from Ryland and stepped into the

kitchen. Cherry cabinets, marble countertops and stainless steel appliances gave the room a darker feel, but it was offset by more windows and an open breakfast nook with a heavy wood table. Michele sat at the table with an older version of Ryland to her right. At her left, another man's back was to Jennalyn.

He was tall and slender, sitting a head higher than Michele. On the lower left side of his hairline, a small patch of gray interrupted his neatly cut brown hair.

"Ryland is here with his friend."

"Jennalyn." Michele smiled as she rose from her chair.

She wasn't the one who captured Jennalyn's attention. No. Jennalyn recognized that patch of hair.

Michele's boyfriend stiffened. So did Jennalyn.

Michele's words and those of Ryland's parents blurred in a buzz of past memories.

"Kris." She didn't make it a question, because she had no doubt that the man keeping his back to her was her ex-fiancé.

"Jennalyn." The man who'd lied to her, cheated and then abandoned her when her life had been at its lowest pushed back from the table and turned. "What a lovely surprise."

"It's a surprise." Her eyes shifted to Michele, who watched them curiously. "I don't know how lovely of one."

She'd liked Ryland's sister enough that she wanted to protect her from pain, but she remembered what Ryland had said in the car. Michele had been seeing Kris for a year and a half. Kris had walked out barely over a year earlier.

She'd wondered what she would feel if she ever saw him again. She'd expected outrage or betrayal. Now, with the moment facing her, she felt nothing she'd thought she would.

There was anger, but it was because someone she'd come to like, care about, had been lied to. Ryland didn't like Michele's boyfriend. He wanted to protect his sister from getting hurt, but was in the tough position of overprotective brother who couldn't intrude.

Jennalyn wasn't in the same position. She didn't want to ruin everyone's Christmas or hurt Michele, but she had a strong desire to protect Michele from a life with an ass.

"You know each other?" Ryland asked as he stepped in behind Jennalyn. His hand came to rest at the base of her back.

Curiosity buffeted her from everyone in the room. Kris's curiosity was different though. His dark eyes, as soulless as they'd ever been, regarded her with a worried dare. She'd always given way beneath his unspoken force, always tried to make things easier for him. He expected the same now.

Then there was Ryland. Standing at her side, his gaze heating her though she didn't look his way. He wanted to know what was going on, but his desire for answers wasn't tainted with darkness the way Kris's was. Ryland wouldn't blame or accuse her. If anything he would be proud of her for being strong.

"You could say that. We were engaged," she answered Ryland's question while shifting her gaze from Kris to Michele. Apologizing with her eyes, hoping Michele saw her inner conflict, Jennalyn went on, "until thirteen months ago."

"Excuse me?" The quietly shocked question came from Michele as she turned to Kris. "You never mentioned being engaged."

"It didn't matter," Kris threw the words out like a dart he hoped would hit a bull's-eye.

"It mattered." Jennalyn stepped away from Ryland, distancing herself from him and his family so it didn't hurt as much when they asked her to leave. She smiled, though, as she looked at Kris. And it was a smile that reached the depths of her soul. "It mattered, because being with you, being left by you when times got tough, taught me something."

"Yeah? What did I teach you?"

His inflated ego swelled at the idea that he'd helped her.

"It taught me how to know a real man when I saw him." As soon as she said it she knew just how she felt about Ryland. And though she wasn't ready to visit him at work on a regular basis, she could handle the demands of his job.

"Wait." Michele stepped between them, looking back and forth. Her gaze stopped on Jennalyn, pleading. "You broke up thirteen months ago?"

Jennalyn winced a little. "Just before Thanksgiving."

Michele turned back to Kris. Her shoulders were tight. Her head was high. "You were engaged when we started dating? To Jennalyn?"

"I'm telling you, 'Chele, it didn't matter. She doesn't matter." Kris's sleazy alter ego showed himself.

His eyes darted to Ryland, and Jennalyn understood everything. Kris didn't care about Michele. He cared about her brother's position in the medical industry. He cared about how a marriage to a Davids could further his career.

"Kris." Jennalyn shook her head and enjoyed watching him pale a couple shades. He knew she knew what he'd planned. "That's a new low, even for you."

Ryland took Jennalyn's hand and pulled her behind him. His dad moved around the table and took up the same kind of protective stance in front of Michele. Michele placed a hand on her dad's arm and stepped around him to face Kris directly.

"You should leave." Michele spoke quietly, with a determination and strength Kris wouldn't know how to argue with. "Any man who thinks Jennalyn is nothing isn't worth the oxygen he breathes."

Ryland and their dad stepped forward wearing matching smiles. The coldest, most dangerous smiles she'd ever seen. A shiver ran down Jennalyn's spine as they closed in on Kris and escorted him from the room.

With him gone the tension that had pinched Jennalyn's shoulders eased. Then she looked at Michele and Ellen. Biting her bottom lip, she sought the right words. An apology wasn't enough.

The front door closed with a light bang. Footsteps smacked the wood floors as Ryland and his dad returned. Jennalyn still didn't know how to act or what to say.

She was still trying to figure it out when Michele approached and caught her completely off guard by pulling her into a tight embrace.

"Thank you. I couldn't pinpoint what was wrong with my relationship until you walked in here."

Jennalyn patted Michele's shoulder with the tips of her fingers, not quite confident enough to complete the embrace. "I didn't mean to hurt you."

"You didn't. Oddly, neither did he."

"That's sad isn't it?" Jennalyn chuckled. "You spend over a year with a man and it doesn't hurt when he's gone?"

"It's sad for him." Michele stepped back. Her smile was brilliant, fun and friendly. "The same will never be said for a man like my brother."

"True." Jennalyn smiled at Ryland who stood close behind Michele. "Your brother is impossible not to love."

"Really?" Heat and love radiated from Ryland's eyes and speared deep into Jennalyn's heart as he dared her with his question.

She stepped to him, wrapped her arms around his waist and smiled up at him.

"Sabrina connected me to the world. I lost that connection until you. You've shown me how much I was missing."

"JJ."

Everything around her faded as she looked into Ryland's eyes. It didn't matter that Michele had just broken off a long-term relationship. It didn't matter that Ryland's parents watched. Jennalyn only cared about the man standing in front of her with his hands resting on her hips. "How can I not love the man who helped me rediscover Christmas magic?"

"You can't." He laughed as he swung her into his arms. "It was all part of my master plan."

About the Author

Heart-stopping puppy chases, childhood melodrama and the aborted hangings of innocent toys are all in a day's work for Nikki Duncan. This athletic equestrian turned reluctant homemaker turned daring author is drawn to the siren song of a fresh storyline.

Nikki plots murder and mayhem over breakfast, scandalous exposés at lunch and the sensual turn of phrase after dinner. Nevertheless, it is the pleasurable excitement and anticipation of unraveling her character's motivation that drives her to write long past the witching hour.

Whether it's romantic suspense or contemporary romance with a focus on the lovers, the only anxiety and apprehension haunting this author comes from pondering the mysterious outcome of her latest twist.

Learn more about Nikki by visiting her website at www.nikkiduncan.com. Nikki is also on Facebook and Twitter at nduncanwriter.

A love prescription so potent only the hottest doctor can fill it.

Paging Dr. Hot
© *2012 Sophia Knightly*

Miami TV reporter Francesca Lake is on a manhunt...or rather, a doctor hunt. Frankie wasn't always a hypochondriac. Her motto used to be "Fear is not an option", but everything changed with her mom's near-fatal heart attack. Now a day doesn't go by where she isn't worried about *something*.

After a harrowing incident in the hospital ER, she has a life-altering epiphany. She needs to find a marriage-minded doctor ASAP—one who will calm her fears so she can get on with her life.

So begins a series of amorous escapades and startling revelations as she works her way through the list of eligibles: an outrageous Aussie sex therapist, a brilliant neurosurgeon (who's wired the wrong way), and a handsome Cuban cardiologist.

None of them compares to hunky Dr. Harrison Taylor...but there's a problem. Much as Harrison's rugged physique, forest-green eyes and warm smile make her senses wobbly, she needs a people doctor, not the vet for her miniature dachshund Romeo. Besides, Harrison's propensity for crazy stunts would only make her worry more.

Frankie is trying to be sensible, but her heart and her outspoken dog are conspiring against her...

Warning: Contains juicy secrets and romantic misadventures between a loveable hypochondriac and three hot doctors. Side effects may include intense yearnings for a strong doctor, an adorable miniature dachshund, and an impromptu trip to Miami.

Available now in ebook and print from Samhain Publishing.

Romance

HORROR

www.samhainpublishing.com